Arthur Nesky values control and order in his life. Imagine his frustration when he finds himself the focus of a stalker. After a close call, he visits a friend up north, hoping to get away from his pursuer and gain some perspective. Meeting a sexy man who lights up every nerve ending in Arthur's body is the epitome of bad timing. Then he finds out who Kaiser is . . . and the secrets he holds . . . making him wonder if he's jumped out of the frying pan and into the fire.

Kaiser Roush is nearly three hundred years old, the alpha of his pod, and a successful businessman. Over the years, he's learned the value of hard work, how to make harder choices, and what it takes to overcome the odds. When Kaiser meets Arthur Nesky, his mate, it comes as no surprise that there will be obstacles to overcome.

Even if Kaiser can get Arthur to accept his nature, can he discover and remove the stalker threat as well?

Tangling with a Colossal Squid
Copyright © 2020 Charlie Richards
ISBN: 978-1-4874-2825-9
Cover art by Angela Waters

Published by eXtasy Books Inc or
Devine Destinies, an imprint of eXtasy Books Inc

Look for us online at:
www.eXtasybooks.com or www.devinedestinies.com

Tangling with a Colossal Squid
Beneath Aquatica's Waves: Book Seven

By

Charlie Richards

DEDICATION

For those of you who asked for a little tentacle play . . . Your wish . . . My command. Enjoy!

CHAPTER ONE

Arthur Nesky gritted his teeth, barely holding his temper in check. Yelling at the damn cop wouldn't do him any good.

"That's correct, Officer Branson," Arthur stated, repeating himself for the third time. "I did not recognize the man who attempted to yank me into the alley."

Only his training in martial arts had saved Arthur. Most people wouldn't tangle with a fit, six-foot-one man, such as himself, but Arthur had been getting *gifts* from a stranger for months. He was damn certain his stalker had just tried to make his move.

Now, if I can get this dumb fucker to understand that.

"And you told him to release you, and he didn't?" the cop pressed, his pen poised over his pad of paper.

"Yes." Arthur crossed his arms over his chest, feeling the tug of his suit jacket.

"And then what happened, Mister Nesky?" Officer Branson asked.

Arthur noticed he hadn't bothered to write down anything he'd said.

Narrowing his eyes, Arthur barely managed to bite back his growl. "How many times must I repeat myself before you write down my statement, Officer Branson?" He cast a pointed look toward the nearly blank pad. So far, he was certain the officer had only written down his name.

Officer Branson's cheeks took on a pinkish hue as he lifted the hand which held the pen, palm out, as if in placation. "I'm

1

just trying to get a clear view of what happened, Mister Nesky," the man said, his tone taking on a conciliatory note. "Accusing someone of kidnapping is serious, and if we're wrong, it can have long-lasting repercussions . . . for everyone."

Deciding he'd had enough of Officer Branson's disbelief, he pulled out his phone. He held the other man's gaze as he dialed a number. When he saw the officer open his mouth while narrowing his eyes, he held up a single finger in a *one moment* gesture.

"Hello, Detective Mirrins. I'm sorry to call you so late, but something happened this evening that I believe is connected to your case."

"It's no problem at all, Mister Nesky," Detective Giardino Mirrins assured. "Did you receive another gift or message? How can I help?"

"Not another gift or note," Arthur replied as he steadily held Officer Branson's gaze, watching the man's face turn a darker shade. "A man tried to put a cloth over my face and drag me into an alley."

"Fuck!" the detective cried, and Arthur heard something thud through the line. "Where are you? At the hospital? I'll be right there."

Arthur heard the sound of footsteps thumping on stairs, and he smiled. *This is the reaction an officer should have to an attempted kidnapping.* "Not the hospital, fortunately," he told the detective. "I'm in front of Barney's Bar and Grill on Center Street." Arthur lifted one eyebrow imperiously as he gave Officer Branson a haughty look. "I'm being interviewed by a gentleman by the name of Officer Branson, but I felt certain you'd be interested in knowing a change has happened in your case."

"Damn right I am," Detective Mirrins grumbled. "I'll be right there."

"Thank you." After hearing another grunt through the line, Arthur hung up. He slid the device into his pocket while continuing to hold the officer's gaze. To his pleasure, he could practically feel the indignation rolling off the man. "Detective Mirrins will be here shortly. I believe I'll wait to finish giving my statement until then."

A muscle ticked in Officer Branson's jaw. "That's your right."

Arthur nodded once, then turned his focus to the paramedic that had been hovering nearby the entire time. While they'd been talking, the man had checked his blood-pressure and had taken pictures of the bruises on Arthur's upper arm. He'd even used a swab to clean away the fluid traces around Arthur's nose, which had been left behind by the rag the man had attempted to keep pressed against his face.

"My head is ringing," Arthur admitted. "Is that normal?"

The paramedic smiled, his expression one of reassurance. "After getting attacked and almost abducted, yeah." He nodded. "But it was actually caused by the residual traces of the chloroform clinging to your skin." Holding up a damp cloth, he advised, "Wipe your face, Mister Nesky. Then I'll give you something for the pain."

Even as Arthur took the cloth and obeyed, he stated, "I don't need pain meds. I'm fine." Arthur refused to take anything that might dull his senses while he had to deal with the police, no matter how much his head ached. "I'll take some *aspirin* when I get home."

"Are you certain, sir?" The paramedic didn't seem convinced. "I can offer you —"

"No, really," Arthur cut in, holding up his hand. "I'll be fine until I get home."

The paramedic nodded, then turned to make notes on his clipboard.

"Am I free to go, then?" Arthur asked, redrawing the man's

attention.

After a second of hesitation, the paramedic stated, "To confirm, you are declining further medical attention?"

Realizing the man needed an out, Arthur nodded. "Yes, thank you." He offered the uneasy-looking fellow a tight smile. "As you've confirmed that my condition is not life-threatening, I do indeed decline further medical attention."

Smiling in obvious relief, the paramedic jotted something on the chart, then hopped from the back. "Then, yes." He held up his hand, offering assistance to leave the vehicle. "You are free to go."

Arthur wasn't too proud to take the man's hand. Gripping it, he eased down the steps of the vehicle. "Thank you."

Then Arthur headed toward his own sedan. He pulled open the driver's door and eased behind the wheel. Just as he laid his head against the headrest and allowed his eyelids to slide to half-mast, Officer Branson appeared in the doorway.

"Mister Nesky, I'm sorry, but you can't leave, yet."

Arthur bit back a growl.

God, box of rocks for a brain.

Curving his lips into a scowl, Arthur frowned at the ignorant man. He had no idea how this man had managed to graduate the police academy. Perhaps that year, they were desperate for recruits.

"As you overheard, Officer Branson, I told Detective Mirrins what happened and where I am," Arthur reminded him. "You should have surmised that I'm waiting for him to arrive. After that, I'll give him my statement, since I already have a file open with him."

Officer Branson's eyes narrowed. His lips tightened, pinching flatly. For the briefest of seconds, his top lip curled before he managed to clear his expression.

"I see," the officer stated, his tone bordering on frosty. "In that case, I'm going to assume your call was a false—"

"Mister Nesky!"

Saved by the bell.

"Yes, Detective Mirrins," Arthur called back, still holding the officer's gaze. "Thank you so much for coming."

"Of course," the detective replied, striding into view. "With the issues you've been dealing with, your safety should be everyone's top priority." He cast a scathing look the officer's way. "Hello again, Officer Branson."

Huh. Guess they have history.

"Detective Mirrins." The officer gave the detective a narrow-eyed scowl. "This isn't your jurisdiction. How'd you get here so fast?"

Smirking, Detective Mirrins stated, "I was visiting my mother." Turning his attention back to Arthur, he pulled out a notebook that Arthur had seen many times before. "Please, tell me what happened."

Although Arthur found going through the tale once again annoying, he did it. After all, he didn't trust Officer Branson to reiterate his story honestly. To that end, Arthur shared what had happened — his visit to a bar to meet with a couple of friends, his decision to leave early since Noah couldn't shut up about his boyfriend, and Jacob had wandered away to seduce a guy sitting at the bar, and the subsequent attack by the overweight, dark-haired stranger.

As Arthur described how he'd jabbed his elbow into his attacker's beer gut, then grabbed the pinky on the hand the man held his arm with, yanking back as hard as he could, Detective Mirrins' lips twitched. "Think you broke his finger? Really?" He cocked his head. "How do you know?" Then his brows furrowed. "And where did you learn that?"

"I practice tai chi for relaxation purposes," Arthur explained. "Although when I started when I was twelve, it was because I wanted to be the next *Jackie Chan*."

Detective Mirrins chuckled as he nodded. "Okay, then." After a moment of silence where he jotted several notes onto his pad, he met Arthur's gaze again. "Normally, I'm not one to tell someone to run from his problems, but in this case, is there somewhere you can go?"

"You want me to run and hide?" That was the last thing Arthur thought the detective would advise. "Really?"

"Not run and hide. A vacation." Shaking his head, Detective Mirrins used his pen to point in various directions. "There are cameras here. I'm suggesting a little time out of sight so I can pull footage, run facial recognition, and see if I can find a hit on anyone from your past."

Arthur bit back a growl. His head hurt enough. Besides, he could see the wisdom in that.

Nodding slowly, Arthur murmured, "Okay. A vacation."

Except, where the hell should I go?

Then Arthur remembered a friend who, a couple of years before, had moved from town — Kane Cornshun. Before leaving, however, he'd extended an open invitation to check out his new home.

Guess it's time I take him up on that.

Upon hearing William's snort, Kaiser Roush turned and arched his left eyebrow as he took in his younger brother's amused expression.

"What?"

As if I even need to ask.

Kaiser knew why William grinned broadly at him as he drew closer. His brother's gaze swept up and down his body. He was clearly taking in Kaiser's outfit and hair.

Normally, Kaiser wore either a business suit or fine jeans and a sports coat over a button-down. Today, however, his attire consisted of a pair of worn and faded denim shorts, a butterfly-yellow t-shirt with a silly slogan on it — *no need to repeat yourself, I ignored you just fine the first time.* Kaiser also wore sandals, of which he wasn't a fan. To top it off, he'd pulled his thick black hair — which he usually kept carefully slicked from his face—into a man-bun at the back of his head.

It all fit with the persona he was going for—a laid-back beach bum.

Hell, most everyone he knew wouldn't recognize him if it wasn't for his scent. Fortunately, he wasn't going undercover to investigate a shifter or other paranormal. No, he was going to uncover the truth about the rumors he'd overheard of bullying by human employees at their main cantina in the marine park.

"You're right, Kaiser," William stated, continuing to smirk as he drew close and stopped next to him. "I wouldn't know you if I didn't know you." He touched his nose, indicating his sense of smell. "And no human who's employed with us will recognize you, either."

"That's the plan." Kaiser had gotten the idea of going undercover from a reality TV show. "I'll sort out which human is bullying the others." Turning back to his reflection in the mirror, he grumbled, "It would be so much easier if one of them would tell us the truth."

"Too bad you can't pull the alpha card and force the issue, eh?" William smiled as he bumped his shoulder into Kaiser's. "But since it's not one of ours causing the trouble, and whichever human is doing it is damn discreet and the others won't rat on him, well—" His brother shrugged, although his expression appeared a little troubled. While Kaiser nodded, William added, "I just don't understand it."

Sighing deeply, Kaiser nodded once. "Me, neither." Turning to face William, he held his brother's gaze. "But we'll get this sorted. We won't allow some asshole human to undermine the safety and comfort we've created here at *World of Aquatica*."

"Damn straight," William replied, a snarl sinking into his tone. Then he grinned broadly and slapped Kaiser on his upper arm. "Well, all right then." A second later, his features hardened — not something that happened often on Kaiser's fun-loving, relaxed, younger brother . . . especially since the shifter had found his mate. "I've put out the feelers to everyone in the pod that they're not to reveal who you are. They'll be treating you just like a regular customer."

Kaiser scoffed softly, betraying his disbelief. While he figured the members of his pod would try, they wouldn't be able to pull it off completely. That was just the way a pod worked.

As the alpha, all of Kaiser's people deferred to him. He was the boss. His word was law.

Some alphas took complete advantage of that, but Kaiser was not one of them. He took the care and keeping of every member of his pod as a serious duty. When their kind — shifters of many aquatic and semi-aquatic species — had opened the doors to their marine park — *World of Aquatica* — they'd become an even larger success than they thought they would. They'd expanded.

That meant hiring more and more humans that didn't know about shifters.

Kaiser still felt responsible for their well-being . . . at least while the humans were on their grounds.

With that thought in mind, Kaiser returned his focus to his brother and curved his lips into a smirk. "I'll be off then." He patted the other man's upper back before sauntering toward the door and beckoning over his shoulder. "Thanks for your help with putting this outfit together."

William chuckled softly as he fell into step beside him. "You got it, Kaiser." He winked before sweeping his gaze over Kaiser's form again. "No way you could have pulled off that look on your own."

Kaiser growled softly as he scowled at his brother. "Shut up," he grumbled, barely resisting the desire to scrub his hands through his hair. He couldn't remember the last time he'd pulled his hair up. Instead, Kaiser patted the man-bun to make certain it was still in place as he muttered, "Hope this doesn't take long. Not certain how long I'll be able to keep from tearing this damn thing out of my hair."

Barking a laugh, William reached past him and grabbed the door's handle just beyond him. "Let's get your assignment started, then."

More than onboard with that, Kaiser exited his top floor apartment suite. There were only two on this level of the condominium building, and William shared the other side of the floor with his human mate, Captain John Casinov. The strait-laced, rugged human was a great addition to their pod, giving Kaiser access to John's connections on the force. Plus, he stabilized William's carefree nature.

And I am in no way jealous that my younger brother found his mate before me.

Pushing that thought from his mind, Kaiser nodded as he and his brother headed from their home.

"As soon as I learn anything, I'll call you," Kaiser promised.

William gave him a thumbs up, then spun off and strode in another direction.

Kaiser strolled toward the diner that his people had told him most of the rumors originated — *Shark Bites and Burgers Cantina.*

CHAPTER TWO

"This place really is amazing," Arthur commented as he strolled through the massive marine park beside Kane. At one time, the handsome graphic designer had had a crush on him, but that was long past. Now, Kane only had eyes for his husband—Tortelion Muenster, Tort to his friends. Arthur smiled at Tort. "Thank you for giving me a tour."

Tort nodded, grinning. "Sure thing, buddy." The laid-back, dark-haired man had his arm slung around Kane's shoulders while using the other hand to point out any and everything. "Any friend of Kane's is a friend of mine." Then he winked as he added, "Besides, it gives me an excuse to stick close to my man while his hot boss who he used to have a crush on is in town."

"Tort!" Kane gasped, his pale cheeks instantly flaring to a crimson shade. "Damn it!" While peering at Arthur with a side-eyed look, he muttered, "I'm so sorry."

Arthur couldn't help himself. He tipped his head back and laughed. His mirth was so great that he ceased watching where he was going and bumped into someone.

Still grinning, Arthur focused on the guy, ready to apologize. Then he damn near swallowed his tongue. While Arthur didn't usually go for the beach bum type, the man before him totally rocked his ragged cut-off jean shorts that showed off his tanned, lightly-haired, and muscular legs. Plus, the form-fitting t-shirt—which had a slogan reading, *last clean t-shirt*—accentuated the man's six-pack abdominals.

Wow! Hot damn!

Arthur realized he was practically drooling over the stranger's sexy frame, so he yanked his focus upward. That didn't help much. The guy sported wide strong-looking shoulders. Even the way his black hair was pulled into a man-bun on top of his head didn't hide his aristocratic features.

His fingers twitching, Arthur had a sudden desire to grab the man's hairband and yank it from his head. He wondered what the guy's dark locks would look like flowing around his shoulders. Arthur wanted to know how far down they reached.

"Hi, there." The man's deep voice cut into Arthur's thoughts. Lifting a hand, the guy touched his jaw lightly in a way that Arthur found almost as intimate as a kiss. "And who might you be?"

"Hey, Al, um, Kaiser," Tort greeted the stranger. "Uh, how's it goin'? What's shakin'?"

Upon hearing the hesitation and correction done by Kane's big, self-assured husband, Arthur managed to jerk his gaze away from the sexy surfer dude before him. He took in Tort's furrowed brows and the tension in his shoulders. Considering the man had been nothing but laid-back and confident, Arthur wondered why he suddenly had a bout of stress over a beach bum.

Unless he's a druggie or a known troublemaker?

"Just comin' for lunch," Kaiser replied, a small smile curving his lips. "Was gonna talk to Sharon, then get some food." Drawing his hand away from Arthur, he focused on Tort. "Join me for a sec, huh?" Then Kaiser turned his attention to Kane. "Order me the chili cheese fries, would ya?"

"Of course," Kane immediately replied, nodding. Without missing a beat, as if taking orders from a guy dressed as a sand rat wasn't anything new, he grinned at Tort. "You want the bacon double cheeseburger, like usual?"

Tort's gray eyes lit up. "Ahhh, you know me so well." Then he dipped his head and pecked a kiss to Kane's lips. "And a beer, babe."

Kane nodded, looking supremely happy. "You got it."

For a second, Kaiser stared at Arthur. His deep green eyes gleamed in the sunlight, some hidden desire swirling in their depths. Then he reached out and touched Arthur's chin again before taking a step backward and opening the door to the restaurant.

Once everyone had entered the huge, cafeteria-style establishment, Kaiser cast one more long look at Arthur, then headed off. Tort joined him, following. Kane gripped Arthur's upper arm and urged him toward the order line.

"So, um—" Kane nibbled his bottom lip as he glanced around furtively. When he met Arthur's gaze again, a smirk curved his lips. "You got a thing for beach bums I never knew about? Or just Kaiser?"

"Uhhhh—"

Arthur rubbed the back of his neck, feeling uncomfortable. He couldn't remember the last time someone had so bluntly asked about his interests. As a successful businessman in San Diego, he was afforded a measure of respect.

Evidently, Arthur accepting Kane's offer to visit meant he was treated a little differently. So far, he'd enjoyed that. Of course, never would he have thought Kane would so bluntly ask about who he might be interested in.

Never thought I'd literally bump into a guy that would make my blood sing in my veins, either.

Clearing his throat, Arthur met Kane's gaze. "Actually, his type has never interested me before, but—" He paused, trying to put into words what he was feeling.

Kane beat him to it.

"Kaiser has that *one thing*, right?" Kane's dark eyes took on a knowing gleam. "That one thing that will push past all other concerns or inhibitions. It makes you want to talk to someone that you wouldn't normally talk to. Right?"

Arthur narrowed his eyes as he processed Kane's comments. They were surprisingly astute. His responses to Kaiser were exactly that.

It didn't matter that Arthur had always been able to peruse a beach bum's tanned toned body with appreciative dispassion. He couldn't do the same to Kaiser. With Kaiser, he wanted to touch and explore.

That burning desire coursed through his body and caused his fingers to twitch. His blood had heated and flowed south, and even now, he struggled with getting his semi to go down. He didn't understand it, and for someone who valued control over most everything else, that was a problem.

Especially since he currently had a stalker after him.

Wait a minute. What if Kaiser is my stalker?

The man didn't look anything like the guy who'd tried to kidnap him the week before, but that didn't mean much.

What if Kaiser had paid that guy?

As Arthur placed his order with the lady behind the counter, unease curled in his gut. Even though he'd been hungry just five minutes before, he suddenly wasn't certain if he would be able to eat a bite.

Kaiser practically vibrated with shock, and the desire burning through his veins made thinking clearly difficult. Never, in all his nearly three hundred years, had he thought it possible to respond to someone in such a visceral way. After watching the way others had bent over backward to woo and claim their mates, Kaiser really should have known better.

My mate. God, I've met my mate!

"Uh, Alpha, why did you want me to join you?"

Tort's question drew Kaiser's thoughts back to where they should be — finishing his undercover assignment. As much as he wanted to stick close to his mate, to learn everything about him and woo him, he had a job to finish first. Good thing he'd finally figured out what was going on. His upcoming chat with Sharon was just the final nail in Edward's coffin — metaphorically speaking.

"What's the name of the man you and Kane are dining with?" Kaiser asked bluntly. He pulled out his phone, preparing to shoot a quick text to Ovram, a sea lion shifter who was their pod's technical genius. While finding out about the man from himself would probably be the gentlemanly thing to do, Kaiser's squid urged him to do everything in his power to expedite the process of learning about his mate so they could bond with him.

Besides, Kaiser wasn't known for being a gentleman. He was known for his ruthless business tactics and his controlling nature. Kaiser would discover how to win his mate, then do it.

"His name is Arthur Nesky," Tort told him, cocking his head. "Kane met him when Arthur became a client at his old job. When Kane moved here and opened his own business, Arthur retained his services." Shrugging his shoulders, Tort continued, "They're friends, sort of, I guess."

"Sort of, you guess?" Kaiser pressed, typing a quick message to Ovram. "What's that supposed to mean?"

Tort shrugged again. "Well, before yesterday, I always got the impression that they kept most of their conversations to work with a little superficial *how are you* and *how's married life treating you* shit." Rubbing his fingers through his hair, Tort added, "I was a little surprised when Kane told me that Arthur was finally taking him up on his offer to show him around if he came up to visit."

"Well, I'm glad he did." Kaiser saw the confusion flicker across Tort's face, so he decided to throw the man a bone. "Arthur Nesky is my mate."

"Oh, wow! Damn!" came the fellow shifter's not-surprising response. When Kaiser arched one brow, he quickly amended, "I mean, congratulations." Tort reached out and touched Kaiser's upper arm for an instant before shoving his hands in his pockets. "Really. Congrats. It's just, Arthur lives in San Diego. I think he owns some kind of engineering firm down there. Something big and important to the city. Works with city planners, I heard, anyway."

Kaiser hummed, nodding. "I see. It may be difficult to extricate him from the city." Rubbing his hand over his jaw, he narrowed his eyes as he swept his gaze over the huge cafeteria-style eatery. Kaiser spotted Kane and Arthur at one of the order stations and realized he needed to get a move on. "Fate doesn't make mistakes," he stated confidently. Resting his hand on Tort's shoulder, he squeezed lightly as he gave the tiger shark shifter a feral smile. "Especially with the help of friends."

Tort grinned back. "You're always there for us. You know we'll be there for you." Pulling away, he waggled his eyebrows. "I'll go talk ya up. Make ya sound good."

Chuckling under his breath, Kaiser nodded. "Thanks."

After Tort had moved away, Kaiser sauntered toward the hallway leading to the restrooms as well as one of the doors to the restaurant's inner workings. He had told everyone that he was going to see Sharon, which was true. What he hadn't mentioned was that he was going to see several others, too.

Kaiser stopped outside a door marked *employees only* and leaned against the wall. Shoving his hands in his pockets, he tipped his chin down. With his acute shifter hearing, Kaiser easily made out every footstep and every voice in the room on the other side . . . which was a small breakroom for the employees.

The other side of the breakroom had a storage area with lockers for them to leave their personal items. There were locks on both doors, but Kaiser had a passkey. As the owner of the marine park, he could get in anywhere he wanted.

"Trade Saturday shifts with me, Sharon," someone male demanded. "I don't wanna work 'til closing."

"I can't, Edward," Sharon replied, tension in her tone. "I specially asked for my shift to end at four because it's my mother's sixtieth birthday on Saturday. She's having a big party, and family have been coming in from other states for it."

Edward snorted, and when he replied, it was with derision. "As if I care about your mother or family." Kaiser heard footsteps, and he guessed the man was advancing on Sharon when he heard lighter footfalls moving away from the heavier ones. "I want your shift, and you're gonna give it to me."

"No," Sharon replied, although her voice wobbled. "I won't."

"Yeah, you will," Edward taunted. "Or I'll tell Uncle Jeremy that you're sexually harassing me. I'll get you fired and take your shift anyway."

Kaiser knew that Edward's Uncle Jeremy was one of the managers at the cantina. His shift was due to start in less than twenty minutes, and William would be meeting with him beforehand. To Kaiser, the timing was critical to clear out the riff-raff.

Sharon gasped. "You wouldn't."

Edward laughed, the sound one of cocky pleasure. "Sure would." His voice darkened. "I always get what I want, Sharon. You should know that by now."

Having heard enough, Kaiser pulled his hands from his pockets, drawing out his keycard in the process. He swiped the piece of plastic through the reader as he heard Sharon reply, "Are you really that selfish? My family has been planning this for months."

Before Edward could reply, Kaiser sauntered into the room. He swept his gaze over the space, taking in Edward's smug smirk as he eyed Sharon, which matched the scent of satisfaction he emanated. Sharon, on the other hand, smelled of unease and frustration, and her cheeks were pale while her eyes were wide.

"Evening," Kaiser greeted, glancing between them. "I happen to know Jamison is managing at the moment." He was supposed to be replaced by Jeremy, but Kaiser had already called in a replacement. "I'd like to see him."

"I'm sorry, sir." Edward stepped forward, puffing out his chest a bit as he twisted his features into a firm expression. "Customers can't be in here." He pointed at the door behind Kaiser and stated forcefully, "Please wait out in the dining floor, and we'll bring our manager out shortly."

Kaiser lifted one brow as he stared down at the human. The blond stood just shy of six feet with a slightly chunky frame, and he had a few pockmarks on his face, indicating he'd fought a nasty bout of acne at some point in his past. At six-foot-four with wide shoulders and a muscular body, Kaiser easily outweighed him and towered over him.

Gods, the human is either cock-sure or just stupid.

Probably both.

Dismissing Edward for the moment, Kaiser focused on Sharon. "Would you fetch Jamison, please, Sharon?"

Sharon's head bobbed. "Yes, Mister Roush." Then she scurried from the room.

By the time Kaiser refocused on Edward, the human's face had bleached of color. Evidently, he recognized the name. Kaiser pinned what he knew was a haughty stare on the bullying human.

"I-I'm so sorry, sir," Edward began, obviously stammering to save face. "I didn't recognize you." He rushed to one of the nicer chairs in the breakroom, a padded one backed against a wall beside an end table. "Please, have a seat, sir. I'm sure Sharon will only be a minute." Smiling in what appeared to be an almost simpering expression—which Kaiser found really weird on the young man—Edward eased forward and bounced on his toes. "Can I get you a drink or a snack from one of the vending machines?"

Kaiser sauntered toward the chair Edward had indicated as he replied, "No, thank you." He pointed at a nearby chair that was facing a table. "Have a seat, Edward." Then Kaiser settled on his chair, stretched his legs out in front of him, and crossed his sandal-clad feet at his ankles.

As Edward did as Kaiser had ordered, he furrowed his brows. "You know my name, Mister Roush?" Cocking his head, he gave Kaiser a sly smile. "Is that because you're interested in something I can help you with?" Edward licked his lips as his focus drifted to Kaiser's crotch. "Are you asking for my manager because you need to borrow me for a while?"

Kaiser felt as if his skin crawled. It had been a long time since he'd been propositioned so blatantly by someone he found so distasteful. He suddenly missed his power suit something fierce.

There was something about the expression *the clothes make the man.*

So damn true.

Dismissing that, Kaiser scowled at Edward. "No." When Edward opened his mouth, he gruffly ordered, "Stay silent."

Edward snapped his mouth shut, but his expression screamed mutinous. The young human was obviously not pleased by Kaiser's dismissal.

Too damn bad.

Fortunately, in the next instant, Jamison strode into the room, followed closely by Sharon. Kaiser smiled at the young woman. "Thank you, Sharon. That will be all." She nodded once, then scurried from the room.

Kaiser had no desire for Sharon to remain. After all, that would just peg a target on her back. Doing it this way, Kaiser hoped that Edward never found out who had convinced the others to speak out against Edward and his uncle.

"Mister Roush?" Jamison appeared surprised, but as a lobster shifter, he could use scent to confirm that it was indeed his alpha who sat before him. "I, uh . . ." He glanced at Edward, then returned his attention to Kaiser. "How may I be of assistance, sir?"

Pulling out his phone, Kaiser tapped it as he spoke. "You are, of course, aware of our zero tolerance for bullying policy," he stated, then held out his phone. "We have a situation."

Jamison took the phone and began scrolling through the contents. His face began to pale. He glanced furtively at Kaiser, then at Edward, before refocusing on the phone.

Kaiser knew what the man was reading. He'd compiled a list of complaints and statements from other employees about Edward's behavior. There were also reports of how Jeremy had ignored them.

Clearing his throat, Jamison straightened to his full height. "I see, Alpha." Then he turned and focused on Edward. "I'm sorry, Edward, but in the face of these reports, I'm left with no choice. Please hang up your apron and clear out your locker. I'll calculate your final check and have it to you in fifteen minutes."

His face turning bright red, Edward leaped to his feet. "What the hell? You can't do that!"

Giving the young human a cold smile, Kaiser stated, "I assure you, Edward. I can."

CHAPTER THREE

"I'm sorry." Arthur held up his hand, causing Tort to fall silent. "Did you just tell me Kaiser and his brother are majority owners of this place?"

That made no sense to Arthur, whatsoever. The handsome man had been dressed as a beach bum, after all. What kind of business owner did that?

Tort nodded. "He is."

He sounded so confident and certain.

Huh.

Processing that, Arthur picked up one of his French fries and swiped it through his ketchup. He popped it into his mouth and chewed slowly. As he enjoyed the salty potato treat — something he rarely indulged in, but seeing as he was on vacation — he glanced between Tort and Kane.

Kane nodded, too. "He's telling the truth," his friend assured. "He's" — he paused, opening then closing his mouth, before finally finishing — "I was gonna say a good guy, but I'm not certain that would apply."

"Kane," Tort hissed, staring at him with a scandalized expression on his face.

Rolling his eyes, Kane continued, "Well, I'm not gonna lie. Even for the alpha." He picked up his burger and nudged his shoulder into Tort's. "Besides, I'm happy saying he's an amazing businessman, a good al, uh, *leader*, and the best man to have in your corner."

"How does that make him not a good man?"

"Well . . ." Kane began slowly, clearly searching for words.

"I think what Kane is trying to say" — Kaiser's voice interrupted Kane's fumbling explanation right before said man slid into the booth seat beside Arthur — "that even though I do everything in my considerable power to help and take care of those under my authority, I'm pushy, dominant, and like to get my way."

On instinct, Arthur slid over further to make more room, even though he'd thought he'd left plenty when he'd first sat down. When first finding seats, he'd pointed at a table with four chairs, but they hadn't reached it in time. There were other open ones across the room, but Tort had guided Kane toward the booths near the front windows, instead.

Arthur had had no choice but to follow. Well, unless he wanted to make a scene or eat alone. That would have been hard to explain.

Kaiser seemed to take up all the space Arthur offered and then some, pressing his thigh against his own. The hairs on his leg stood on end, and his body warmed. He felt tingles erupt on his skin, spreading outward from where Kaiser touched him.

Pushy, dominant, and likes to get his way.

Tilting his head, Arthur glanced pointedly at where Kaiser blatantly pressed against him. "You don't say."

Kaiser chuckled, then picked up a fry drenched in chili and cheese. After slinging his left arm along the back of the bench seat, he popped the gooey mess into his mouth. Teasing the fingers of his left hand along Arthur's shoulder, Kaiser winked.

Arthur tensed in his seat, then forced himself to relax. He refused to allow the pushy bastard to ruffle him. After all, he managed to wheel and deal with politicians and city officials. Arthur knew he could handle another businessman, regardless of his status — or how he dressed.

Instead, Arthur picked up his hot dog, which he'd laden with mayonnaise and ketchup, as he eyed Kaiser. When he'd seen the traditional offering of a footlong with a basket of fries, he hadn't been able to help himself. Arthur couldn't actually remember when he'd last been on vacation and indulged in such a thing.

Before taking a bite, Arthur swept his gaze over Kaiser's t-shirt and shorts-covered frame again. Then he met the man's deep green eyes and asked, "Are you on vacation, too?" Unable to help himself, after taking a bite, he hummed. The flavor of the dog mixed with the bun as well as the hefty coating of mayo and ketchup, and he enjoyed it immensely. Arthur knew the footlong was so damn unhealthy, but it still tasted so fantastic.

Gonna pay for this later, but wow!

The marine park's cantina didn't disappoint.

"No," Kaiser answered. As he picked up several chili cheese fries together, balancing the chunks of meat and goopy cheese carefully, he added, "Actually, I'm undercover. Just figured out who was bullying some of my employees and fired his ass." There wasn't a hint of remorse in his face or tone as he leaned forward over his plate and took a careful bite of his food. Around his mouthful of food, Kaiser added, "Got rid of his asshole uncle, too, since he was complicit in his nephew's bullying."

"Like that TV show?" The words were out of Arthur's mouth before he could think better of them.

Kaiser made a humming noise of confirmation as he popped the rest of what he held into his mouth.

"Okay." Arthur really didn't know what else to say.

Evidently, Kaiser didn't have that problem. "So, I know Tort has given you a tour of part of our lovely marine park." His expression turned heated as he offered, "I would be more than happy to show you a little of the behind-the-scenes areas."

Arthur inhaled deeply, a wash of heat thrumming through him. His half-hard prick twitched, threatening to thicken the rest of the way. He shifted in his seat, fighting his urge to adjust himself.

"You're forward," Arthur decided to go with before taking another bite of his food.

"Like I said, pushy, dominant, and I like to get my way," Kaiser reminded as he teased his fingertips up the side of Arthur's neck. "You're a handsome man, Arthur. You know that, too." Smiling heatedly, Kaiser told him, "It's not often I meet a man who piques my desire so instantly, and I know you recognize our chemistry." His voice turned husky as he leaned closer and finished on a whisper, "It would be foolish to squander such a rare and glorious opportunity."

Arthur nearly choked on his next bite of hotdog. He put down his half-finished food and grabbed his water glass. Coughing under his breath, he brought the straw to his lips.

After several deep gulps of the refreshing liquid, Arthur scowled at Kaiser. "No more suggestive remarks until after we finish eating," he ordered. To Arthur's surprise, Kaiser dipped his head in acknowledgment.

Kaiser didn't stop touching him, though. Lightly skimming the backs of his fingers up and down Arthur's neck, he grabbed some more fries. "So, Arthur, what brings you to our marine park?"

For a second, Arthur hesitated.

Should I tell this man the truth? Can I trust him?

Arthur had never trusted instantly before, so he didn't understand his sudden urge to do so now. Of course, he had always trusted his instincts, too. This man obviously wanted to fuck him, and Arthur knew he'd never crossed paths with him in the past.

I would have remembered an instant chemistry connection like this.

That meant Kaiser wasn't his stalker.

"Hmmm." Kaiser settled his hand on Arthur's nape, cradling it in a light massaging hold. "There's a story there." Narrowing his eyes as he tipped his head to the side, Kaiser's dark eyes glittered as he focused intently on him. "You don't have to tell me now, but I hope soon, you'll trust me with it."

Arthur found himself nodding.

"Then let's move on to another subject." Kaiser grabbed a couple more fries, and before popping them into his mouth, he asked, "Have you seen the tiger shark show?" He pointed at the clock. "The next show starts in twenty minutes."

"It was sold out," Tort stated, amusement that Arthur didn't understand filling his tone.

Kaiser snorted. "As if that would stop me." He refocused on Arthur. "If we hurry and eat our fries on the go, I think we can make it."

Arthur thought about the show he'd been disappointed had been sold out for the afternoon. Having read about how the marine park handlers had somehow trained a tiger shark to show off for a crowd, he had hoped to see it. Still, when Tort had offered to get them in anyway, since he was an employee of the park, he hadn't wanted to take someone else's seat.

With Kaiser asking the same thing, Arthur couldn't resist twice. He had been second-guessing his decision all afternoon, after all. Arthur nodded.

"I'd like that."

Kaiser's grin appeared almost self-satisfied. "Then eat your dog, my mate, and we'll get to walking." After that, he turned and focused on his chili fries, leaving Arthur confused by the odd endearment.

Kaiser enjoyed watching the wonder on Arthur's face more than watching the show. He figured that was partly due to the fact that he'd seen it more than a few times and knew that the tiger shark was actually a shifter named Caden. Along with him, Tort and a third tiger shark shifter named River traded off, putting on the shows.

On top of that, Kaiser was learning little tidbits about his mate. For example, he knew the man enjoyed meat, because when a hunk of dripping pork had hung above the pool, and the announcer—Gerald—had made a joke about pork ribs, Arthur had hummed, then muttered, "Yum," under his breath and laughed. He'd also licked his lips.

After another part of Gerald's speech, where he talked about safe practices for swimming with sharks, Arthur had mumbled under his breath, "Damn, that would be so cool."

Kaiser absently wondered if his mate would feel the same about swimming with a massive squid. His animal lowed in his mind, and he mentally agreed. He couldn't wait to find out.

By the time they were done watching the show—which Kaiser and Arthur had enjoyed from a private box reserved for very special occasions, such as wooing mates—his human was relaxed and smiling.

"Can I show you some of the behind-the-scenes happenings?" Kaiser asked, hoping to get Arthur away from the main crowds. He wanted to spend a little time with him in a more discreet setting, and he knew his fellow shifters would steer clear of him with just a look. "I could show you some of the medical areas or private pools used for integrating new fish or other species into our aquariums."

"Really?" Arthur seemed surprised. "You were serious about that?"

Nodding, Kaiser did his best to keep his lust from his expression. "Of course." He tipped his head toward the door. "I'm proud of the work we do here, and I'm happy to share it with someone I'm interested in."

"Interested in?" Arthur's tone took on a teasing note. "Really?" As he strode toward the door, he peered over his shoulder with a smirk curving his lips. "Sure you don't mean a guy you want to fuck?"

Growling under his breath, Kaiser stalked after Arthur. He grabbed his mate's arm and jerked him close so that he could duck his head and whisper, "I want to do more than fuck you, Arthur." Kaiser couldn't help the admission. Misunderstandings between mates never worked out well. Upon seeing Arthur's eyes widen, Kaiser slid his other arm around his back and tugged him tight against him. "I intend to make love and worship every inch of your gorgeous body."

Then Kaiser gave in to his baser instincts. He dipped his head and sealed his lips over Arthur's. Swiping his tongue out over his mate's bottom lip, he groaned upon tasting the slightly salty — probably from the fries — and masculine taste of Arthur's flesh. Kaiser lost himself and pushed his tongue between his human's lips.

For several long moments, Kaiser submerged his senses in the delicious taste of everything Arthur. He swept his tongue around his mate's cavity, mapping and learning. When he gently guided the other man's tongue into his mouth so he could suckle lightly, Arthur moaned into his mouth and vibrated in his arms.

Only Kaiser's need to breathe caused him to finally break the kiss.

Kaiser panted harshly. His blood hummed in his veins, and his cock throbbed in his shorts. A shiver of need pulsed through his body, and he struggled to control himself.

Resting his forehead against Arthur's own, Kaiser groaned softly. "Damn, baby," he muttered. "The things you make me feel." He sighed deeply.

To Kaiser's satisfaction, he felt an answering tremble in Arthur's body. His mate was just as affected.

Good. Gonna take advantage of that pull.

After inhaling deeply, the scent laced with Arthur's musk and arousal, Kaiser groaned softly. He lifted his head and gave the other man a rueful smile. "We better get out of here before I lay you over one of these seats and pound your ass."

Arthur groaned, even as he stepped away from him. "Damn, the things you say to me." He lifted his hands as if warning Kaiser back. "Yeah. Yeah, we should definitely get out of here." His cheeks were flushed as he shoved his hands into the pockets of his jeans. "Time to head somewhere where there might be some supervision."

While Kaiser didn't believe that would help them in the least, he still nodded. "Come on."

To Kaiser's pleasure, Arthur didn't fight him when he took the man's hand and led him down the steps. He threaded their fingers together, making his hold tighter. His excitement mounted when his human didn't even try to tug away.

Touching him is perfection.

Kaiser just managed to keep from rolling his eyes at his own thoughts. He'd never been a sap before, always down to earth and focused. Finding his mate, however . . . that seemed to bring out all kinds of unexpected emotions.

As they exited the stadium used for several different kinds of marine demonstrations, Kaiser smiled at Arthur. "Come on. Let's head to —"

"Alpha Kaiser!"

Turning, Kaiser swept the crowd, searching for Doc Anthony. He recognized the voice of the hammerhead shark shifter. Doctor Anthony Keller handled the medical end of his pod.

Finally spotting him, Kaiser narrowed his eyes. "Yes, Doctor?" he called, turning and heading toward him. "What is it?"

"It's Vivian," the doc told him, his chest heaving. "I'm so sorry to interrupt, but she came in with mild contractions. She didn't think anything of it, but after twenty minutes of monitoring her, her water broke. She's in early labor."

Kaiser nodded, immediately understanding the problem. "You need her husband, and Niall is in the main exhibit area." He prided himself on knowing every shifter's work schedule if it was part of the park. Resting his hand on the doc's shoulder, Kaiser assured, "I'll pull him out. You get back to Vivian."

"Thank you," the doctor replied, relief in his scent and the slope of his shoulders.

As he began to turn, Kaiser called, "Why didn't you call me?"

Doctor Keller peered over his shoulder at him while still moving. "I did, but it went straight to voicemail. Tort told me where you were when I had Eban send out a pod-wide beep."

"Seriously?" Kaiser grabbed his phone from his pocket. Grimacing, he shook his head. "Fucking hell. I must have hit the silent button at some point. I'm so sorry."

As the alpha, Kaiser should *never* be out of reach, since emergencies, being emergencies, could happen at any time. *Damn.*

Still, as Kaiser headed in another direction, he felt the tug on his hand. He realized he was still pulling his mate behind him. In the face of finding the other half of his soul, Kaiser could accept that he'd make a mistake.

"Is everything okay?" Arthur asked even as he quickened his pace to keep in step with Kaiser's longer stride.

Kaiser nodded even as fear clenched in his gut. "An emergency, but I'll get it sorted." As he moved, he pecked a kiss to his mate's temple and muttered, "Hope you have an open mind."

CHAPTER FOUR

A rthur followed along docilely as Kaiser wended his way along walkways. His heart thudded in his chest as trepidation built within him, but it was beat out by excitement. He wondered what the hell was going on.

And why is Kaiser including me? I'm a complete stranger.

For an instant, Arthur wondered if he was being played. Could all this be some massive ruse by his stalker? As soon as that idea popped into his head, he dismissed it. Just as before, he knew he would have remembered meeting Kaiser.

I need to stop jumping at shadows.

Then what the hell did his comment about having an open mind mean?

When they entered a huge building, went down a slight incline, and entered a massive underwater aquarium, Arthur almost pulled away from Kaiser. He really wanted to stop and take it all in. The creatures within were amazing!

Arthur kept moving one foot in front of the other, however. Somehow, he knew that he would have the chance to see everything again. That was, if he stuck with Kaiser.

When Kaiser used a keycard to open a nearly hidden door, Arthur finally paused. The bigger man must have felt his hesitation, for he turned and focused on him. Without saying a word, Kaiser tugged lightly once more.

"If you wish a true backstage experience, come with me now," Kaiser urged. Then his tone softened as he added, "If you're not ready for something . . . life-changing, then go to Mini Barrier Reef Cantina, and I'll catch up with you when

I'm done here."

Life-changing?

"Is it safe?"

Arthur already had enough life-threatening shit in his life.

Kaiser's eyes narrowed just a smidgen as he cocked his head. "You are completely safe when you're with me," he assured. "I will never allow any harm to befall you."

Seeing the serious—and somewhat questioning—glint in Kaiser's eyes, Arthur dipped his head in a nod. "Okay." He followed the man through the doorway.

As soon as the door shut behind them, Kaiser strode purposefully down the hall and up a set of stairs. At the top was another doorway. He once again used his keycard to open it.

This one opened to a massive cavernous room.

Arthur peered around with wonder even as he hustled after Kaiser. There were metal walkways criss-crossing the space, wending between the different aquariums. Tubing filled with water jutted from the tanks, disappearing into the walls.

He wondered if those were for circulation or had some other use. They were awfully big, after all. In fact, some of them could even fit the largest of sharks.

Perhaps they're used for shunting fish between tanks.

"I need protocol six enacted on tank eighteen," Kaiser bellowed as he strode swiftly through the place. "Now!"

A man in tan slacks and a polo shirt swung around. He gaped at Kaiser, opened his mouth, then inhaled deeply. His cheeks pinked, and his eyes widened.

An instant later, the man crossed to a panel and hit a button. A buzzing sound began, which accompanied the clang and grinding of something moving. A second later, he saw the way a metal shield began sliding into place, covering the viewing glass of one of the far aquariums.

Kaiser moved toward that same aquarium while ordering, "Sweats, t-shirt, and sandals for a medium build." He glared at someone who looked askance at him as he growled, "Move your ass, Kanton. Now!"

The dark-haired guy's eyes widened. A second later, he too sniffed. Then he scurried in the other direction, possibly heading to do what Kaiser had asked.

Once Kaiser reached the side of the aquarium, which was now closed to public viewing, he cocked his head as he stared into the water.

Arthur followed the man's gaze, and his eyes widened. His lips parted as surprise flooded him. To his shock, the water before them was filled with fish, sharks, and other marine life that had been swimming within the aquarium . . . and they were all gathered together and peering up at them.

Looking over his shoulder at him, Kaiser murmured, "Remember, no matter what you see or what happens, you are safe. You will *always* be safe." He squeezed Arthur's hand, then brought it to his lips and kissed it. His gaze simmered as he released Arthur's hand, and he rumbled huskily, "You are my mate, my other half, and I will explain anything and everything . . . shortly."

Then Kaiser knelt on the metal decking and reached out his arm. He appeared to be stretching his limb toward the fish. Except, it didn't stop there. Kaiser's arm stretched and thinned and—

"Oh my god!"

When Kaiser's arm turned gray and split, Arthur couldn't hold in the words. He couldn't believe what he was seeing. No way could it be true.

Did I eat or drink something I shouldn't have? Have I been slipped something? Surely I'm hallucinating!

Arthur still couldn't tear his gaze away from what he watched. Kaiser's arm—*arms?*—had turned long and slender from the elbow down. They sported grayish skin and sucker-like things on the undersides. Kaiser wiggled them through the water, reaching beneath the waves.

The appendages wrapped around a very large tortoise and drew it toward the surface.

To Arthur's continued surprise, the tortoise didn't bother to fight the limbs.

As soon as the animal cleared the water, Kaiser ordered, "Shift, Niall. Your wife needs you."

Watching what happened next, Arthur fell backward, landing on his ass. He gaped. His heart thudded wildly in his chest. His head swam.

"Oh, fuck!" Arthur hissed. Then his eyes rolled to the back of his head, and he welcomed the darkness.

After all, no way could what he'd seen be real. Men did not grow tentacles out of their arms, and turtles did not turn into men. Arthur looked forward to when he woke up.

Then the world will again make sense.

Kaiser noticed Arthur's weaving form and extended his other arm toward him. Shifting his left arm into his tentacles as well, he barely caught him before he toppled into the aquarium behind him. As Kaiser released Niall and returned his arm to his human form, he drew Arthur closer with his left.

Once Kaiser had Arthur pressed against his side, he changed that arm back, too. Fully human again, he cradled his mate against him. Then he returned his focus to Niall, who was pulling on the sweats provided by Kanton.

"Your wife went into premature labor, Niall." Kaiser pointed toward the door. "She's at Doctor Keller's clinic. He's waiting for you."

"Thank you, Alpha." Then Niall shoved his feet into the provided sandals, grabbed the shirt from Kanton, and started rushing away, putting the shirt on as he walked.

"Is he going to be okay, Alpha?" Kanton asked, eyeing Arthur curiously. "He acted like he'd never seen you shift before, but surely you'd never—"

Kaiser narrowed his eyes as he cut off Kanton's suppositions by saying, "This is my mate's first introduction to shifters."

Upon seeing Kanton's eyes widen, irritation burned through his veins. Kaiser hated explaining himself, and Kanton was a worry-wart. The clownfish shifter had a nervous personality, always questioning things and scurrying about making certain every bit of the aquariums were clean and secure.

As much as Kaiser appreciated that trait when it came to Kanton's job as the aquarium keeper, he didn't care for how it showed up in other areas of his life. The man questioned other people's choices constantly. As his alpha, Kanton didn't have the right to do it to him.

"Are you certain that was wise, Alpha?" Kanton asked, shifting from foot to foot as he twisted his fingers before him. "I mean, he didn't seem prepared to see that at all." Cocking his head and leaning closer, Kanton squinted at Arthur. "He passed out from shock. Will he even remember when he wakes up? What if —"

"Kanton, that's enough," Kaiser barked, his irritation morphing into anger. "Do not question how I introduce my mate to paranormals," he snapped. Then he swung his mate into his arms and turned away from the twitchy male. "Reopen the exhibit."

"Oh! Yes, Alpha." Even as Kanton bobbed his head, he gave Arthur another curious look before rushing away. "Right away."

Kaiser shook his head as he started toward a back exit. "Now the fact that I found my mate and he passed out will be around the entire pod within a day," he grumbled. He knew it was his own damn fault, since he hadn't wanted to allow Arthur out of his sight if he could help it. "I'll deal."

Then Kaiser utilized the back alleys of the marine park and

headed home.

When Kaiser pushed through the door of his condo, for an instant, he entertained the idea of taking Arthur straight through to his bedroom. He didn't, although he sure wanted to, knowing that would be far too presumptuous. Instead, Kaiser moved to his living room and laid Arthur on the sofa.

More than ready to get out of his beach bum clothes, Kaiser kicked off his sandals. He wriggled his toes in the carpet as he yanked his t-shirt over his head while heading toward his bedroom. Hearing the sound of Arthur's body moving over the fabric of the couch cushions, he realized his mate was waking.

Kaiser draped his shirt over the back of a reclining chair as he moved back to the sofa.

Arthur's head turned toward him, and his eyelids fluttered.

Settling his butt on the cushion next to Arthur's hip, Kaiser rested his palm on his human's side. He squeezed lightly. At the same time, he rubbed his thumb along the line of Arthur's rib, wishing he was touching skin instead of cloth.

When Arthur's eyelids cracked and he peered up at him, Kaiser smiled. "Hi, handsome. How are you feeling?"

After blinking a couple of times, Arthur glanced around. "Confused," he answered, his voice sounding husky. "Where am I?"

"My condo," Kaiser told him honestly. "I wanted you to have plenty of time to recover after fainting." Plus, he wanted Arthur in his space for the next part of their discussion. "And I figured you would have plenty of questions about what you saw."

Arthur jerked to a sitting position, using his hands to slide backward and away from Kaiser's touch. "You took me to your home?" He glanced around, his scent taking on an acrid flavor, betraying his rising panic.

"Easy. Easy," Kaiser crooned, drawing out the words. "You're not in any danger. You're safe."

"Does that mean you wouldn't try to stop me if I decided to walk out the door?"

Surprised by the question, Kaiser frowned. When he saw Arthur lean away from him even farther, he realized what he was doing. Even though Kaiser's shifter instincts screamed at him to wrap Arthur in his arms and soothe him, he knew that wasn't what was needed.

Kaiser forced his features into a reassuring smile as he eased backward on the sofa, putting more space between them. "If after we talk about a couple of things, you wish to leave, I will not stop you." His gut twisted just saying the words.

He didn't want his mate to leave . . . ever.

Can't say that right now.

Seeing how Arthur had responded to being taken to his home without permission told Kaiser that something was going on with his mate.

When Arthur didn't respond, Kaiser realized what had drawn the man's attention—his bare torso. His human's gaze was focused on his chest, sweeping over his wide shoulders and defined pectorals. When Arthur's attention slipped southward, Kaiser couldn't help but react. His blood flowed south, filling his cock, and his nipples beaded as his chest warmed.

The only thing that would have been better was if Arthur was actually touching him.

Kaiser hated to do it, but he needed information first. Clearing his throat, he drew Arthur's gaze back to his face. Smiling warmly, he winked.

Arthur's cheeks darkened, and the scent of embarrassment filled the air. "Why're you half undressed?" Arthur mumbled, glancing around the room again, only to pause upon seeing Kaiser's bare feet. He once again met Kaiser's eyes. "What's going on?"

"I hate sandals, but wearing them was required for my undercover persona. I ditched them as soon as I walked in," Kaiser revealed, shrugging. Placing his left arm on the back of the sofa, he leaned partly against Arthur's legs and the back cushion. "And I was about to change into something more my speed, but I heard you moving and didn't want you to wake alone." Rubbing his right hand over Arthur's lower leg, Kaiser enjoyed the feel of the rough hairs under his palm. "Will you tell me why you were so concerned about leaving?" Something in the way he'd reacted truly bothered him. "I know what I showed you can seem disturbing, but I assure you, it is completely natural."

Well, for a well-trained alpha shifter, anyway.

Not all shifters had the ability to shift only certain parts of their body. It took a great deal of control, concentration, and years of training. Kaiser had spent decades honing the ability, and he'd spent even more time teaching his brother, William.

Arthur finally relaxed against the cushion behind him. After scrubbing his hands over his face, he sighed deeply. He grimaced as he met Kaiser's gaze again.

"I'm not in the area just for a vacation. I'm here avoiding a stalker."

Kaiser narrowed his eyes as he digested that bit of information. "A stalker?" When Arthur nodded, he urged, "Please, tell me about it. Who is it?"

Lifting his hands in an *I don't know* gesture, Arthur shook his head. "If I knew, it would make things so much easier," he told him. "After the notes, the gifts, and the pictures the stalker has sent, if I knew who it was, I could get a restraining order against him"—after a second of hesitation, Arthur added—"or her."

"Then I will spread the word through the pod to be on

watch for any suspicious activity," Kaiser stated calmly, mentally formulating a plan. "I'm sure the police have the originals, but if you give me copies of the notes and pictures, I can have—"

"Wait, what?" Arthur lifted his hand, palm out. "Why?"

"To find the stalker and remove him from your life." Kaiser thought that would have been obvious.

"But why help me?" Arthur asked, clearly confused. "I mean, sure we have chemistry and a romp between the sheets would be fun, but . . ."

Furrowing his brows, Arthur rubbed the back of his neck as he glanced at Kaiser's still-tented fly. Even talking about a stalker hadn't caused his erection to deflate. Kaiser's body reacted to being close to his mate in a typical shifter response. He wanted the man.

Even with half his blood filling his little head, Kaiser still figured out what Arthur was asking. "Ah. That has to do with what you saw at the aquarium. My arms changing into tentacles to pull Niall from the aquarium, and the tortoise shifting to a man." He grinned, pinning a hungry stare on his mate. "We are shifters. Paranormals. And you, Arthur Nesky, are my mate. The other half of my soul." As Kaiser rubbed his hand up his human's bare calf, then slid it under the hem of his shorts so he could massage his thigh, he added, "I would do anything for you, Arthur, including pleasuring you and taking out any threat to your safety."

CHAPTER FIVE

"Shifters. Paranormals," Arthur mumbled, resting his hands on either side of the bathroom sink. Hanging his head, he allowed his mind to reel. "And I'm his mate."

Over the last hour, Kaiser had explained the paranormal world to Arthur. He had told him how his kind shared their spirit with some kind of animal. Many of the people working at *World of Aquatica* were shifters who could turn into some kind of aquatic or semi-aquatic animal. Nearly all the rest were humans mated to those shifters.

It wasn't until just the past year that the marine park had become so popular and huge that they'd been forced to begin to hire outside humans. That was why Kaiser had needed to go undercover. He'd needed to clear out the problem humans in a way that they couldn't cause human resources problems or sue the company.

"Arthur?" Kaiser knocked softly after calling through the closed door. "Are you okay? Or are you freaking out?"

"Neither," Arthur admitted, speaking quietly. He knew Kaiser would still be able to hear him. Evidently, paranormals were stronger, faster, and had superior senses. "Just taking a minute to process."

"Ah." Kaiser's deep husky chuckle came through. "Understandable. Are you interested in dinner? I can order in."

"How about pizza?" Arthur figured if Kaiser had something to do, he would leave him alone for a few minutes.

"Any toppings you don't like?"

"Anchovies and pineapple."

Kaiser laughed again. "Good. Me, too. Take all the time you need, my mate."

Arthur didn't respond. Instead, he closed the lid of the toilet and sat on it. Resting his head in his hands, he closed his eyes.

Okay. So maybe I am freaking out . . . a little.

Kaiser had offered to take him to a massive underground cavern to show him his colossal squid. Arthur had been damn tempted. The expression *seeing is believing* had come to mind, but then Arthur realized that he already *had* seen.

According to Kaiser, few shifters had the training and discipline to shift only a small part of themselves. As far as Kaiser knew, himself and William, his younger brother, were the only ones in the pod with the skill. Then he'd waggled his eyebrows, given him a heated smile, and told him he could do some pretty extraordinary things with his tentacles.

Arthur had felt his whole body flush as ideas bombarded him. That was when he'd decided to use the bathroom. Now, his cock was hard as a rock, and his body thrummed with need.

Also part of the mate-pull thing.

Evidently, that was part of meeting your paranormal mate, too. They were drawn to each other. The chemistry was explosive, and their need for each other was damn near off the charts until they completed their bond and twined their life-threads.

Then the pair never wanted to be apart for long, and since Kaiser was alpha of his pod, Arthur knew what that meant. The man expected him to leave his life in San Diego and move in with him. Clearly, shifters did things fast.

"Arthur, you've been in there for thirty minutes. The pizza is here."

Lifting his head, Arthur felt his lips part as shock filled him. "Damn. Really?"

"Afraid so."

Arthur pushed to his feet and realized his butt was a little sore from sitting on the hard porcelain for so long. After rubbing his ass cheeks, he took a deep breath, then let it out between pursed lips. He had always faced his problems head-on, and he would treat this no differently.

Although, is finding out I have a soul mate who wants to devote himself to me actually a problem?

Huh. Yes and no.

Because it means a life-change I hadn't considered.

Having learned that Tort was a tiger shark shifter, Arthur finally understood Kane's shift in attitude. He knew the man hadn't been happy at the graphic design firm he'd been working with, but Kane leaving for a man he'd met only a couple of weeks before had surprised Arthur. He felt the same urge, which was what truly scared the shit out of him.

Arthur had always thought through his decisions. He didn't jump in head-first. He analyzed and planned.

"Arthur?"

Realizing he was standing and staring at the door, he grimaced. He pulled his head out of his ass and grabbed the doorknob. Then he opened the door and peered up the couple of inches difference in their heights and met Kaiser's gaze, finding worry in the man's deep green eyes.

Arthur's heartrate sped up in his chest. His body flushed. Heat coursed through his veins.

Kaiser was still shirtless, showing off his expansive torso. He'd removed the man-bun at some point, and his locks were slicked back from his face, falling in waves that framed his masculine features perfectly. His full lips were curved into what looked like a reassuring smile. With the way Kaiser gripped either side of the doorframe, he appeared open and welcoming.

For some reason, Arthur didn't think that was a side of him that Kaiser allowed too many people to see.

But I'm his mate, so I'm different.

Special.

"Hello, Arthur," Kaiser rumbled softly. "How are you doing?"

Arthur took a few seconds to really think about his answer. "I . . . I'll be fine," he answered slowly.

Rubbing the back of his neck, Arthur slid his focus downward, unable to help himself. He admired the view, including the thick ridge filling out the crotch of Kaiser's shorts. His own prick twitched, and Arthur longed to give in to his need . . . but he knew how Kaiser would take that.

Upon feeling Kaiser's crooked forefingers under his chin, Arthur lifted his face.

"The need I see on your face, the need I can smell emanating from you, is making it difficult to think," Kaiser admitted, his tone rough with his own desire. "Would you like to take the edge off? We can eat in bed after."

Arthur wanted that so damn bad, except—"Will that start the bond between us?"

Kaiser's eyes narrowed as he curved his lips into a feral grin. "Yes, because I have every intention of fucking you raw."

The rumbling purr of Kaiser's tone caused goose bumps to rise on Arthur's skin, and the images caused by his words created a spike of need to burn through him. His chute muscles clenched as he thought about milking Kaiser's seed from him, of feeling its warmth within his body. He panted softly as his fingers twitched with his desire to feel the bigger man breeding him.

"Ahhh, you do like the sound of that," Kaiser continued roughly. "You want my seed in you, don't you?" Lowering his hand, he skimmed the backs of his forefingers down his neck. "You want to feel me warming you from the inside out, marking you in the most primal of ways." Then Kaiser scraped a nail over the point where Arthur's neck met his shoulder. "Then I'll mark you on the outside, right here, making you mine forever, and every paranormal will know it."

Arthur found he wanted that, so damn bad.

"B-But I don't live here," Arthur blurted out. "I have a business in San Diego. I—"

Growling softly, Kaiser offered a wide smile. "Plenty of people have a virtual office, Arthur. And my pod owns a helicopter, so when you need to be in San Diego, we'll go. We'll buy a cottage on the ocean."

"Just like that? You'll leave your pod because I have to be in San Diego?" Arthur could hardly believe what he was hearing. "But you're the alpha."

Kaiser tipped his head to the side as he told him, "My brother is my beta, and he's perfectly capable of handling things for a day or two whenever it's needed." Sliding his hand around Arthur's neck, he cradled his nape in a warm hold. "You are my mate, and your needs will always come first."

"You've thought of everything, have you?" Arthur tried to think rationally, but he found himself drowning in Kaiser's touch. The man was so strong, so forceful and dominant, yet he was caring, too. "What about my stalker?"

"We'll find him," Kaiser assured. "Let me help you . . . care for you." He eased closer, brushing his body against Arthur's. "Do what we both want. What we need, my mate."

"You are persuasive," Arthur mumbled on a gasp as he felt Kaiser's other arm wind around his waist. "I've never just jumped in with both feet before, but you make me want to."

Kaiser dipped his head and whispered into his ear, "Then do it. Jump in with me. I vow you won't regret it." Kaiser massaged the small of his back, teasing his fingertips underneath the shirt. "I swear I'll catch you."

Arthur felt a shiver work through his body, and his body burned.

"Yes."

The word was barely out of Arthur's mouth when Kaiser used his hold on his neck to urge him to turn his head. Then the man's lips were on his own, and his tongue was in his mouth. Gripping Kaiser's waist, Arthur gave up the fight and welcomed the bigger man's ravishing.

My mate said yes!

Kaiser knew his dominant persistence was probably pushing Arthur to accept him and their bond faster than the man might be comfortable with. He wasn't above a little seductive persuasion to get what he wanted, however. Besides, Arthur was his mate, his perfect complement, and he would spend his life making certain his human never regretted the decision — even if it was rash.

Hell, we haven't even known each other a half a day.

Dismissing his internal concerns, Kaiser ravished Arthur's mouth. He teased along his tongue, then nipped at his lips. After licking away the sting, he rubbed their lips together lightly before breaking the kiss.

Seeing the stunned, lust-drunk expression on Arthur's face, Kaiser grinned with satisfaction. "So fucking handsome," he rumbled as he began using his hold to maneuver his mate toward his bedroom. "Can't wait to kiss every inch of your body, to leave love marks on your skin."

As Kaiser spoke, he reached behind Arthur. Dipping his head again, he nibbled along the man's neck, relishing the slight salt on his flesh mixed with the flavor of his skin. It made gripping his bedroom's doorknob and turning it tough, but he managed it. He pushed it open, then returned his hand to Arthur's back.

Lifting his head, Kaiser urged Arthur through the doorway. His body burned with a fierce need he'd never before experienced. He practically vibrated with it, his cock throbbing behind his fly.

Kaiser lifted his head and drew a deep breath, struggling to rein in his unraveling control. Seeing Arthur's deep-blue, lust-filled eyes glazed with hunger did little to help. Inhaling slow and deep didn't help, either. All that did was fill his lungs with the delicious scent of Arthur's arousal.

Groaning roughly, Kaiser gripped his soon-to-be forever lover's shirt hem. He tugged it up, eager to reveal his mate's body to his hungry gaze. To his pleasure, Arthur lifted his arms, allowing him to whip it over his head.

Dropping the cloth to the floor, Kaiser eagerly reached for his fly next. "These need to come off," he stated forcefully. "Or I'll tear them from you."

Arthur snorted and pushed his hands away. "Then I'll do it. I happen to like these shorts."

"I like how your ass looks in them," Kaiser countered with a feral grin.

Kaiser obeyed, however, in favor of crossing to his nightstand and grabbing the lube. After tossing the tube onto the bed, he opened his own shorts. He shoved them down and kicked them off. Since Kaiser rarely bothered with underwear, that left him naked, his aching prick jutting from between the black hairs at his groin.

When Kaiser turned, he nearly swallowed his tongue. "Oh, Arthur," he purred, his heart tripping in his chest. "You are absolutely stunning."

Arthur was, too. His strong six-foot-one frame was lean and toned with lightly defined muscles in his limbs, betraying that he took good care of himself. What was even better, however, was the way Arthur stared back at Kaiser, hunger filling his blue eyes.

"On the bed, Arthur," Kaiser demanded, stalking toward him.

Smirking, Arthur crossed his arms over his chest, his stance one of pride. "What if I want your ass first?"

Kaiser froze. In all his long years, that was something he'd never done. With how dominant his personality was, who would top or bottom had never been in question with his prior partners.

But this is my mate.

Swallowing hard, Kaiser nodded once. "If that is what you wish."

Evidently, that wasn't the response Arthur had expected. His jaw sagged open, and his eyes widened. For a second, he just stared.

Then Arthur whispered, "Really?"

"You are my mate, Arthur," Kaiser reminded him. "If you want to top me, then I will gladly give you my body."

For a few seconds, Arthur continued to stare at him. "I wouldn't have expected that," he admitted softly as he cocked his head. "You're obviously a dominant top. I was actually just pulling your leg."

Kaiser hummed as he closed the distance between them. Satisfaction filled him that he'd pleased Arthur with his response. "Well, should you truly feel the need to top me, just say the word." Knowing he had to be truthful with his mate, he continued, "While I've never accepted another into my body, I will for you. All I ask is that you go slow."

Even though the request made him sound like a blushing virgin, the idea of feeling the seven or so inch dick jutting from Arthur's groin caused his chute to clench and trepidation to fill him.

For my mate . . .

"I'll consider it," Arthur told him. Lifting his hands, he settled them on Kaiser's torso, causing goose bumps to break out on his skin. "But as much as I love being the powerhouse in a meeting, in the bedroom, I like to be taken care of in bed." Then his eyelids slid to half-mast, and his smile curved into a hungry smile. "So, take care of me, Kaiser." Arthur stepped forward, closing the scant distance between them, and he rubbed his erection against Kaiser's own. "Your mate needs you."

Kaiser knew he'd never heard words so sweet.

"My mate," Kaiser mumbled on a groan.

Gripping Arthur's waist, Kaiser lifted and turned, tossing his human onto the comforter. He quickly clambered after him, using his knees to nudge the man's legs apart.

As Kaiser gazed at Arthur's strong, toned form, he knew he was the luckiest damn shifter in the world.

CHAPTER SIX

Arthur couldn't remember anyone looking at him the way Kaiser did right then. The feral desire glimmering from the man's dark green eyes made his breath catch in his throat. A tingle traveled across his chest, and his nipples beaded.

When Kaiser levered over him, placing his hands on either side of his shoulders and keeping his weight off of him, Arthur felt the man's erection bump pleasantly against his own. He planted his feet and rocked his hips up. Seeing Kaiser narrow his eyes and offer a feral grin, Arthur did it again, rutting up against him.

"That's the way, my mate," Kaiser rumbled. "Show me what you like."

Without waiting for a response, Kaiser dipped his head and sealed his mouth over Arthur's. The kiss was short and feral, a plundering of teeth, lips, and tongue. It started and ended swiftly, yet still left Arthur breathless.

His entire body vibrated with need for the touch of the man hovering over him.

To Arthur's pleasure, Kaiser began licking and nibbling along his jaw, then down the line of his throat. Enjoying the zings of sensation the man's light five o'clock shadow created, he tipped his head, offering more room. Feeling Kaiser rub his whiskers over his Adam's apple, Arthur let out a husky groan.

"Gods, Arthur," Kaiser mumbled against the flesh of his collarbone. "Love the sounds you make." Then he sucked on the flesh, the move causing the hairs on Arthur's arms to stand on end.

Gripping Kaiser's shoulders, Arthur clung to the big man. He arched under him, rubbing his body against Kaiser's. Sweat broke out on Arthur's skin as Kaiser worked his way down his pectoral.

Kaiser latched onto Arthur's nipple, sending spikes of sweet tingles down his chest. They spread across his groin, and his cock throbbed and twitched. His balls rolled in his sack, and he realized he was embarrassingly close to coming.

"W-Wait," Arthur cried, even as his hips bucked spastically.

When Kaiser lifted his head and peered into his eyes, a question in their depths, Arthur swallowed hard, searching for his voice.

"What is it, Arthur?" Kaiser crooned. Lowering his head even as he continued to hold his gaze, he hummed and rubbed his lips over Arthur's swollen bud but didn't latch back on. Instead, his lips teased at it while Kaiser stated, "Anything you want, my mate."

A shudder worked through Arthur upon hearing those words. He felt the skim of Kaiser's palm over his left side, then the scrape of his nails along his hip. When his new—and forever—lover teased his fingertips into the skin at the apex of his thighs, Arthur's eyes practically rolled into the back of his head.

His cock throbbed even harder, a drop of pre-cum sliding across his ultra-sensitive crown.

"P-Please!" Arthur found himself whining. "Please, p-please."

"Please what, my handsome human?" Kaiser murmured before rubbing his whiskers lightly over Arthur's puckered nub. "Anything. Just tell me."

The pleasure-pain on Arthur's over-stimulated nipple

yanked a moan from his throat. He tightened his grip on Kaiser's shoulders. While he figured he dug his nails into the bigger man's flesh, he couldn't stop himself, and Kaiser didn't say a word of complaint.

"N-Need," Arthur ground out. "C-Come."

"Then come, sweet Arthur," Kaiser urged as he wrapped his long fingers around Arthur's erection. "Paint us with your seed."

The thought that Kaiser was way too coherent passed in and out of Arthur's mind between one heartbeat and the next.

In the next instant, Kaiser jacked him, wiping out any thought Arthur might have had except enjoying the exquisite sensations cascading through his body. His erection twitched beneath his lover's slow jacking caresses. Shudders racked his body.

"That's the way, Arthur," Kaiser encouraged. "Spill your seed. Show me how much my touch turns you inside out." As the shifter spoke, he tightened his grip on Arthur's dick and swiped his thumb over his crown. Just before wrapping his lips around Arthur's nipple and sucking once more, Kaiser whispered, "Love seeing you come undone from my touch."

Arthur couldn't have stopped his orgasm even if he'd tried, which he didn't. Groaning deeply, he shuddered in Kaiser's hold. His erection pulsed as waves of bliss-inducing endorphins crashed over his senses.

"Kaiser!" Arthur cried as he shivered and twitched. His seed warmed his stomach as his pulsing streams splattered over his skin. Upon feeling Kaiser's warm tongue lap over his skin, Arthur moaned his name again. He peeled open his eyelids, uncertain when he'd even closed them, and stared down at the huge man lapping up his cum with a smile on his face and hunger in his eyes. "So fucking sexy."

Flicking his gaze to his face, Kaiser winked. Then he returned his attention to where he cleaned him . . . with his tongue. Arthur found the sensation of Kaiser licking repeatedly to be one of the sweetest feelings he'd ever experienced.

That was about the time Arthur felt something else . . . a finger easing in and out of his ass was joined by a second one. He almost began to clench, due to surprise, since he didn't know when Kaiser had started stretching him. Then the fingers nudged that spot inside him, tearing a fresh moan from his throat.

Kaiser chuckled darkly, drawing Arthur's focus to his face. His lover winked, his expression wicked. "That's the way, my mate. Relax, 'cause I'm gonna fill you up so good."

"Yes!" Arthur called, rocking into the stimulating touches.

Between watching Kaiser clean his stomach with his tongue and feeling the man's fingers stretch his inner muscles, Arthur felt his dick thicken right back up.

Or did it never soften?

When Kaiser pulled his fingers free and reared up between his legs, Arthur realized it didn't matter. Watching his lover grease his bare dick—his bare, thick, and maybe ten-inch cock—getting the huge monster buried deep in his body was all that mattered.

With that one thought in mind, Arthur lifted his legs and rocked, rolling over. Getting his knees under him, he arched and spread his legs.

Upon hearing Kaiser whisper his name, Arthur peered over his shoulder at him. He grinned. The blatant, pain-filled need in the man's eyes almost had Arthur shooting right then.

"Fuck me, Kaiser."

"Yesssss!"

Kaiser didn't disappoint.

Kaiser had never seen a prettier sight—his mate on his knees, presenting his ass, and begging for his cock.

Stunning.

Unable to resist the siren call of his mate's body, Kaiser draped over him. He gripped the base of his dick in one hand while carrying his weight with his other. Then he guided his crown to Arthur's stretched and lubed hole . . . and pushed.

Groaning harshly, Kaiser shuddered upon feeling the exquisite squeeze that clamped down on his cock head. He barely stayed the urge to slam home, driving himself as deeply into his human as possible. Instead, reminding himself that he was a big man, Kaiser froze.

Arthur moaned and shook, his hot chute muscles fluttering around Kaiser's flared crown.

Kaiser gritted his teeth as he dipped his head and nuzzled the man. "Easy," he managed to get out. "Just relax."

To Kaiser's surprise, Arthur peered over his shoulder and snapped, "I'll relax when you're balls deep and reaming my ass. Now fucking fuck me already!"

"Oh, gods!" Kaiser couldn't stop the words as he took in the needy gleam of Arthur's blue eyes, dark with passion, and the desire etched onto his features. "Yes, my mate!"

While Kaiser bit back his instinctual words of reassurance, the desire to say that his mate's wish was his command, he did obey. He listened to Arthur's words, and he thrust forward. Kaiser let out a deep bellow of delight as he sank his aching shaft deep, deep into his human's welcoming body.

Kaiser bottomed out. His groin hairs rubbed against the soft swell of Arthur's exquisite cheeks. He couldn't resist peering down to view where he was embedded inside the other man.

Seeing how his thick erection stretched Arthur's ring caused a shudder to work through him. His prick also jerked where it was buried inside his lover. Nothing had ever appeared so sexy . . . or felt so exquisite.

My mate, my human, my Arthur.

With his need to make that a reality, to spill in his Arthur, to bite him and bond them, Kaiser started moving. He pulled his prick nearly free, reveling in the feel of the edges of his crown being teased by the muscled ring of his mate's opening. When Arthur groaned his name and arched his back, pushing back toward him, Kaiser let loose his baser instincts.

Curving over Arthur's back, Kaiser wrapped his right arm around his mate's torso. He gripped him to his chest as he slammed forward again. Hearing Arthur's feral cry of delight, he grinned and did it again . . . and again.

Kaiser knew he nailed Arthur's prostate on each glide by the way his human shook in his arms. Scenting the delicious aroma of his lover's arousal caused his senses to sing. Kaiser's body damn near vibrated as he sank to the hilt in Arthur over and over, and his sweet mate took it all and bucked back against him, searching for more.

With his balls churning with his imminent release and his canines aching, his need to mark his mate inside and out, Kaiser opened his mouth and wrapped his jaws around the flesh of Arthur's shoulder. At the same time, he gripped his mate's erection and began jacking in earnest. To Kaiser's satisfaction, the chute muscles encasing his shaft rippled, expressing Arthur's delight as surely as the man's howl of pleasure.

In the next instant, Kaiser groaned his own bliss upon feeling Arthur's channel clamp onto his dick. He thrust in deep, wanting to feel it all. At the same time, he continued to milk his mate's prick, coaxing every last burst of seed from him.

As soon as Kaiser felt Arthur's orgasm begin to wind down, he relaxed the stranglehold he had on his own pleasure. His balls pulled tight, and his dick throbbed. His release coursed through him, and heady endorphins caused dark spots to dance across his vision.

Kaiser felt the urging of his squid, and he didn't even try to suppress it. Sinking his teeth into the flesh he gripped, he buried his canines deep. Blood welled up around his teeth, and he heard a barked cry—a sound of surprise more than anything. Then the body clutched in his arms shuddered once before a keen of ecstasy filled the room.

Growling his enjoyment, Kaiser swallowed the blood that had filled his mouth. The way the iron-rich, life-giving fluid coated his taste buds sent his senses soaring. Needing more, he sucked on the wound, filling his mouth with more.

When his moaning mate's arms gave out, threatening to take them both crashing to the mattress, Kaiser tightened his hold and held them up. He eased his teeth from Arthur's shoulder, then licked over the wound, sealing it. At the same time, Kaiser eased them to their sides, keeping his sexy man out of the wet spot even as he remained buried in his lover's channel.

Sighing deeply, Kaiser nuzzled Arthur's nape as he rubbed over Arthur's chest. "Damn," he murmured, licking the sweat from his human's skin. "You are so amazing, my mate. Thank you."

Arthur remained silent for a few minutes, and Kaiser began to think he'd fallen asleep. Then a low chuckle filled the room. Surprised, and a little confused, Kaiser levered up a little so he could peer into Arthur's face.

"My mate?" Kaiser pressed a kiss to Arthur's jaw. "Are you okay?"

Arthur opened his eyes and turned his head. His blue eyes gleamed in the dim light of the room. With his lips kiss-swollen, his skin flushed, and his hair wild, Kaiser thought the human looked like a debauched angel.

Gorgeous.

"More than okay," Arthur murmured, smiling at him. Then he chuckled before admitting, "Although, never in a million years did I think that, when I came here to get away, I would end up in the arms of a sexy man, let alone bonded with a shifter." Furrowing his eyebrows, Arthur let out a deep breath as he relaxed on the bed. "I guess I'm going to be going through a lot of changes soon."

Easing his hips backward, Kaiser slipped his softening dick from Arthur's body. He pecked a kiss to his mate's lips, then whispered, "You relax. I'll get something to clean you up." After sliding his fingertips along Arthur's jawline, Kaiser told him, "And I'll do the best I can to make these transitions as smooth and easy as I can."

Kaiser held Arthur's gaze, patiently waiting, until he spotted the small smile curving his mate's lips. Then the human nodded. Taking that as acceptance, Kaiser eased from the bed and padded to the bathroom.

After dampening a washcloth, Kaiser cleaned himself up. Then he tossed it in the hamper. He wet a hand towel next. After ringing it out, he grabbed a towel, then headed back to the bedroom.

As Kaiser drew nearer, he enjoyed the view of Arthur's lean lines. His mate's skin, from his shoulders to his pectorals, was marked with Kaiser's love bites. He could barely wait to deepen the marks and cover the rest of his unblemished skin.

His cock even twitched at the thought.

Spotting Arthur's tired smile, Kaiser realized now was not the time to start another round. His mate needed rest and food, not necessarily in that order. Easing one knee onto his bed, he leaned toward his lover and quickly cleaned him up.

"Just relax, Arthur," Kaiser urged, rubbing the damp cloth over him, clearing all traces of fluid and slick. Then he wiped him down with the dry towel. "I'm going to toss a few pieces of pizza in the microwave to get us started and warm the rest of the pizza in the oven. Do you want a beer to go with it?"

To his amusement, Kaiser heard Arthur's stomach growl.

Arthur rolled his eyes, then used his hands to sit up. "Guess food would be good. And a beer. Yeah." He grabbed a couple of pillows and shoved them behind his back, resting against the headboard. "Then maybe I'll figure out what questions I should be asking about how shifters and their mates work out differences."

Kaiser wondered what kind of differences they could possibly have, but he didn't ask. Hell, the question slipped from his mind as his gaze was snagged by the arresting view. His mate lounged against the headboard. One leg was straight out, and he had the other crooked up, resting his arm on his knee. To Kaiser's pleasure, Arthur appeared completely comfortable with his nudity.

Laughing, Arthur snapped his fingers a couple of times.

Chuckling back, Kaiser shrugged as he met his gaze, grinning unabashedly. "You're sexy."

"Thank you," Arthur replied. Then his smile turned imperious. "Now feed me."

After offering a bow, Kaiser exited the room. He did as he'd said, turning the oven to a low setting. After placing a couple of slices on a paper plate, he slid the rest of the pizza onto a baking stone. That he placed into the oven. He put the plate into the microwave and fired it up.

While the microwave ran, Kaiser crossed to the refrigerator and pulled out a couple bottles of water as well as a couple of beers. He pulled a little-used breakfast tray from his pantry and placed them on it. Then he grabbed napkins. Finally, once the microwave beeped, he added the plate of pizza.

Then Kaiser returned to the bedroom.

Kaiser walked in the door to the sight of a pale Arthur hanging up his phone. Concerned, he placed the tray across his naked mate's lap as he asked, "What's wrong?"

Arthur met his gaze, his deep blue eyes sporting a haunted expression. "I've received another gift from my stalker."

CHAPTER SEVEN

"Why didn't you tell us you were having trouble with a stalker?" Jacob crossed his arms over his chest and scowled at Arthur. "We could have helped."

Noah nodded, furrowing his eyebrows as he pushed up his glasses. "We never woulda let ya leave the bar alone if we knew someone was after you."

Before Arthur could thank his friends, Jacob waved a hand, indicating Kaiser, who sat next to him. "And how do you know this guy ain't your stalker?"

Arthur sighed, resting his hands on his dining room table as he glanced between his friends. He'd asked the pair there for dinner so he could introduce them to his new significant other. They'd been happy for him, until he'd shared the other reason he'd invited them—explaining about his stalker.

"While you have no reason to trust me, I'm not Arthur's stalker," Kaiser stated mildly. Then he turned his attention to Arthur and gave him a lecherous smile. "Although, I guess I will be now."

Butterflies bounced in Arthur's belly just from that look alone, and tingles danced up his spine. His blood rushed south, and his dick plumped.

Giving Kaiser a mock scowl, Arthur grumbled, "Behave." Then he crossed his arms over his chest. "And I haven't agreed to this plan, you know."

Kaiser reached over and gripped his wrist, making him uncross his arms. Then he threaded their fingers together. He squeezed once, then rested their hands on the table.

"I know you don't like my idea, and in truth, I'm not a fan, either. I don't like the idea of putting you in danger." Kaiser sighed deeply, and his lips pinched, expressing his displeasure. "But we need to draw this bastard out."

"What plan?" Noah cut in, glancing from their hands to their faces. Turning his head, he focused on Jacob as he waved toward their fingers. "And no way is this guy the stalker. Stalkers try to extricate their prey from their friends, not include them in their plans." Noah returned his focus to Kaiser and asked again, "So, what plan?"

Realizing the decision truly was out of his hands, Arthur sighed. "Okay, so while I was up north visiting Kane and meeting Kaiser"—he tipped his chin toward his lover and kept talking—"my stalker stole the neighbor's cat and butchered it." Arthur grimaced as he recalled the graphic pictures Detective Mirrins had sent him. "There was a note in the box, too. It said, *if you don't return soon, this will happen to your friends*. Then there was a picture of the three of us from when we were at the bar a week ago."

Damn. Has it only been a week?

Cutting a sideways glance Kaiser's way, Arthur realized he'd only known the man for two days, and he already felt so comfortable with him, depended on him, even.

As if sensing his thoughts, Kaiser smiled at him. "Change can come at you fast."

Arthur nodded. "Yes, it can."

Jacob grabbed his beer off the table and took a swig. "So he's threatening us. Okay." He nudged Noah and stated, "We'll be careful, right?"

Noah nodded.

"I'm quite certain that once we start showing ourselves around town as a couple," Kaiser cut in. "The stalker's focus will shift to me." Holding up his free hand to keep Jacob from speaking, since he'd opened his mouth, Kaiser added, "However, just to be on the safe side, I'm going to assign each of you a bodyguard until this is resolved."

"A bodyguard?" Noah took off his glasses and began using his shirt to clean them. "I think that's a little excessive."

Arthur knew Noah was annoyed and trying to hide it. Cleaning his glasses was a nervous tick. His buddy was a private person, and he wouldn't appreciate having someone in his space, even for his safety.

Reaching across the table, Arthur touched Noah's shoulder. "Please consider it, Noah."

Noah's lips pinched, and a mutinous expression took over his features.

Jacob's lips, however, curved into a roguish grin. "Will my bodyguard be hot?" Leaning over, he playfully punched Noah's upper arm. "This could be fun. You did just break up with Nathan, after all."

"You did?" Arthur realized he'd missed a few things while away for a week. "When did that happen?" He'd only met the blond once, but he'd seemed so into Noah. "What happened?"

"Wednesday night," Noah replied, returning his glasses to his nose. He shrugged as he picked up his beer. "Just didn't work out. It happens."

Arthur knew there was more to the story, but he didn't have time to wheedle it out of his private friend right then. Instead, he stated, "Well, I met the guys who are going to be watching out for you, and they're certainly good looking." Upon hearing a low growl, Arthur snapped his attention to Kaiser. He couldn't help but smirk when he spotted the jealous gleam in his lover's green eyes. "Not nearly as hot as you, of course."

"You shouldn't be checking out other men, my mate." Kaiser used their twined fingers to tug Arthur toward him. "You're mine."

As if to make his point, Kaiser turned in his chair and

slipped his other hand around Arthur's nape. He tugged him close and sealed their mouths together. When Kaiser slid his tongue along Arthur's lips, he opened happily to him.

Arthur gave in to his plundering. As he teased his tongue alongside Kaiser's, he rested his free hand on his lover's thigh. Feeling the thick bunching of muscle there, a fissure of arousal danced across his nerve endings. He tightened his grip, wishing he could feel that solid muscle without fabric between them.

"Woo, woo, woo! Someone call the fire department."

Jacob's teasing words reminded Arthur that they had an audience. It must have clued in Kaiser, too, for he eased the kiss to an end. After one more peck to Arthur's lips, he eased his hold on his neck and straightened in his chair.

A very smug smile curved Kaiser's lips as he eyed him.

Arthur felt his cheeks heat as he straightened, too. Then he needed to adjust his dick behind his fly.

Laughing, Jacob shook his head. "Possessive much, man?"

"Yes," Kaiser replied, completely unabashed. Just as quickly, he returned to the prior subject. "Now then, you will meet Westram and Dare later. They'll be bringing Chinese take-out for dinner." He smirked as he focused on Jacob. "And if you want to fuck, that's totally up to you guys. Just know that both men will put duty before pleasure."

Jacob grinned broadly. "Nice!"

"You are such a horn-dog," Noah muttered, shaking his head. "So who is *your* bodyguard then?"

"His name is Pisces," Kaiser told them. "He'll be joining us shortly, too."

"How come they didn't just come with you?" Noah asked, cocking his head.

"I wanted to explain the situation first," Arthur told his friends. "I needed you to understand how serious this is."

Noah nodded while Jacob stood and crossed to the kitchen

and the fridge. "More beer, anyone?" After getting confirmations from them all, he began rooting around in the fridge. "So, Kaiser," he began, not looking at them. "What are you going to do to get the stalker's focus on you?"

Kaiser waited until Jacob had straightened and was returning to them before he answered. Grinning widely, he claimed, "Public displays of affection."

Jacob barked a laugh as his attention turned to Arthur. "You?" he questioned, setting down the beers. "PDAs?"

Arthur felt his cheeks heat as he grimaced and rolled one shoulder in a half-shrug. "Guess so."

"Not a fan of public displays, Arthur?" Kaiser lifted their twined fingers and lightly nipped Arthur's knuckle, then kissed it, soothing the sting.

Shifting in his seat, Arthur sighed deeply. "Not really," he admitted. "I believe that what two people do in a relationship should be private between them." Then he smiled at his lover. "But I'll manage."

"I'd like to see that, actually," Noah muttered, grabbing a fresh beer.

Arthur scowled at his friend. "Thanks for the vote of confidence."

Jacob snickered as he twisted the cap off his own bottle. "Well, come on, man." He tossed the cap onto the table. "The most we've ever seen you do is hold a guy's hand until two minutes ago," he claimed, referencing the make-out he'd just done with Kaiser. "You're repressed, man."

"I am not!" Arthur cried.

At the same time, Kaiser stated, "Oh, don't worry. I'll loosen him up."

Upon hearing the innuendo in Kaiser's tone, a shiver worked down Arthur's spine. With the way his lover stared at him, he felt the sudden urge to kiss him again. The idea of straddling his lap and grinding against him sounded good, too, even with his friends sitting across the table.

Huh. Maybe PDAs with Kaiser won't be so hard after all.

Kaiser didn't tell Arthur, but he didn't like his plan any better than his mate did. Okay, some aspects of it he looked forward to. After all, Kaiser loved announcing to the world that Arthur was his and his alone.

His squid was possessive like that.

What Kaiser hated was putting a target on Arthur. He knew he would be able to take out some obsessed human. That didn't concern him. Instead, Kaiser feared that showing they were a couple would push the stalker over the edge, and he would go after Arthur, instead.

To that end, Kaiser made certain Pisces knew to stick close to Arthur's side if Kaiser wasn't there. The bottle-nosed dolphin shifter was one of the best trackers in their pod. While following something through water didn't always translate directly to land-based tracking, Pisces had never had any trouble finding his mark.

That meant Pisces would be able to follow Arthur regardless of where he went.

Over the course of the week, Kaiser and Arthur made a production of going to see sea-side homes for sale. He pretty much always kept in contact with his mate, holding his hand, pressing his palm to his back, or wrapping his arm around his waist. The realtor, a petite brunette who somehow managed to get around in stiletto heels, had called them, *such a cute couple.*

Arthur had blushed, which Kaiser found adorable.

While walking in and out of Arthur's condo, they spoke loudly about the homes they were visiting and what features they liked or disliked. They'd even made an announcement about how they were headed to pick out furniture together once they chose a home. Then two days later, they'd done it.

During everything, Pisces joined them. They referred to him as Kaiser's cousin, who was in from out of town to help them move. They even met up with Noah, Jacob, Westram, and Dare on several occasions — at bars and restaurants.

Once while Kaiser walked past Jacob, he'd scented Dare on him. He barely resisted the urge to laugh. It seemed the sensual redhead had managed to get the big, giant octopus shifter to fuck him.

The third time they met with Arthur's friends was at a gay bar that sported a small dance floor.

Before Kaiser could talk Arthur into taking a spin on the dance floor with him, he noticed the tension between Noah and Westram. He took the opportunity of heading to the bar to order more drinks to pull the longnosed saw-shark shifter aside. Resting his hand on the muscular, gray-haired shifter's back, he questioned him.

Westram groaned softly, rubbing his palm over his face. "Noah is my mate." He whispered the admission.

"Shouldn't congratulations be in order?" Kaiser murmured back as they waited for the bartender to get to them.

"You'd think," Westram replied, his shoulders drooping. "But he just broke up with some douchebag asshole, and his self-esteem is shot. Any time I make even a small advance, Noah practically runs." Rubbing the back of his neck, Westram met Kaiser's gaze, sadness filling the gray eyes that matched his shoulder-length hair. "I don't know how to convince him that my interest is genuine."

"Did he make any indication as to why he thinks you're not serious?" Kaiser asked curiously, then turned and gave their drink orders to the bartender before refocusing on Westram.

Westram sighed deeply, shoving his hands into his pockets. "You remember that day we first showed up and Jacob made a comment about wanting to be fucked?"

Kaiser snorted as he nodded. The human was a horn-dog.

"Well, recognizing Noah's scent as mine, I let my little head do the talking." Westram crossed his arms over his chest and hunched his shoulders, as if a six-foot-three, heavily built shifter could become smaller. "I pointed him in the direction of Dare, then turned to Noah and said, *You, on the other hand, are just the kinda man I look for when I want a roll in the hay. You up for one?*"

Cringing, Kaiser shook his head. "So he thought you wanted a hook-up, like Jacob and Dare are doing."

"Yeah." Westram hefted the pitcher of beer as well as the fruity drink they'd ordered for Noah. "And it doesn't help that Jacob talks blatantly about how Dare is fucking him so good, and he keeps encouraging Noah to take advantage of me while he can."

Nodding, Kaiser picked up another pitcher of beer—that one full of a darker brew. "Ouch."

"Right. Plus, no matter how he describes it, I think that relationship he just got out of was a little toxic," Westram told him. "And it doesn't help that I live several hours to the north."

"Once we have this shit sorted with the stalker, ask Noah out on a real date," Kaiser advised. "That man is going to need a slow hand."

"So much for jumping in with both feet like your Arthur," Westram grumbled.

Kaiser chuckled softly as he nodded, offering one more bit of support, since they were nearing the table. "You won't be alone in this, Westram. You know that."

Westram nodded. "Thank you, Alpha."

Once they'd dropped off the drinks, Kaiser turned to Arthur and held out his hand. "I would very much like to dance, handsome." He wiggled his fingers. "Care to take a spin around the dance floor with me?"

Arthur hesitated. Then, to Kaiser's delight, he took his

hand.

Kaiser led the way to the dance floor, keeping them near the edge, so their bodyguard could keep an eye on them. Unable to help himself, after he'd wrapped his arms around Arthur, he slid his right hand into the back of Arthur's relaxed-fit blue jeans. Squeezing the man's globe, Kaiser grinned upon hearing Arthur's gasp and seeing his lips part in surprise.

Sliding his left hand up and down Arthur's spine, Kaiser began swaying with the music. "Love your ass, my mate," he purred as he dipped his head. "But I love something else more." He pressed a light peck to his lips, then nuzzled along his jawline. "And I have something in mind that you'll enjoy very much."

Gripping the back of Kaiser's shirt, Arthur shivered in his hold. "Yeah? What's that?"

Enjoying the breathy quality of Arthur's voice, Kaiser gave in to his need. He concentrated just a little and, under the cover of having it down Arthur's pants, shifted his hand. His tentacles grew from his fingers, and he slithered them between Arthur's ass cheeks.

Arthur gasped and tensed. "What are you doing?"

"Experimenting with your control," Kaiser answered honestly. Giving Arthur a lecherous grin, he added, "And enjoying your sexy body."

Then Kaiser pushed the tip of one of his tentacles into Arthur's chute.

CHAPTER EIGHT

"Oh my fucking god," Arthur hissed. He stared up at Kaiser in shock, trembling, frozen on the dance floor, as . . . *something* moved within him. "Wh-What?"

"Move, my mate," Kaiser encouraged, using the hand on his back to tug him tight against him. Since Kaiser swayed to the music, that meant Arthur began moving, too. "That's the way."

As if I have a choice.

Then whatever the fuck was in him pushed further up his channel, only to ease back out again. It brushed against his prostate, sending spikes of sensation to erupt within his body. He trembled, stumbling, but Kaiser kept him upright.

"Kaiser." Arthur would forever deny the whine in his voice as he felt that thing push against his prostate again. "What?"

Kaiser dipped his head, putting his mouth against Arthur's ear. "You're just fine, Arthur. I promise. That's one of my tentacles playing inside your body."

"What the fuck?" Arthur burst out.

Chuckling huskily, Kaiser suckled Arthur's earlobe, which created a new dynamic of sensation, causing the hairs on his nape to stand on end. The . . . *tentacle* skimmed across his prostate again. Tingles settled in Arthur's balls, combining with the zings Kaiser's mouth caused.

"K-Kaiser," Arthur whined, shivering in his hold.

Kaiser released his earlobe and whispered, "Yes, my mate?"

"We're in public." Arthur grunted as the tentacle pressed

on his internal button again, spiking heat through his entire groin. "Oh my god!" he squeaked. Resting his forehead on Kaiser's collarbone, Arthur tightened his grip in the back of his lover's dress shirt. "Fuck!"

"You smell so damn good when you're aroused," Kaiser rumbled into Arthur's ear, the sound barely able to be heard over the sound of the music. "I would keep you hard and twitching for days on end, if I knew it wouldn't cause you harm."

Arthur whined as he rolled his head back and forth on Kaiser's torso. "Why are you torturing me?" he whined, shivering hard as he clung to his lover. "Th-Thought you w-were" — feeling the tentacle slide over his prostate again, he hissed — "s-supposed to please me."

"Are you not enjoying this?" Kaiser asked huskily.

As Kaiser spoke, Arthur felt the tentacle begin to slide out of him.

Kaiser tightened his arm around Arthur's waist, keeping him close as they moved. "I can stop."

When Arthur's chute was stretched only a little, he finally moaned. "Don't," he pleaded, bucking his hips. "Pl-Please don't stop."

Growling softly, Kaiser nipped his neck. "Your wish." He moved his tentacle deeper again, the appendage swirling, stretching, and pushing within his body. "My command."

Arthur had to grit his teeth to keep from shouting with bliss. His dick was so hard it hurt, and he knew he leaked behind the zipper of his jeans. With each step that Kaiser encouraged him to take, the damp cotton of his boxer-briefs rubbed over his flared head, sending zings of blissful fire to his balls.

When Arthur's testicles began to tighten and the telltale tingle at the base of his spine formed, he gasped. "K-Kaiser," he whined, shivering. Snapping his eyelids open, he finally lifted his head and peered up at Kaiser. "Gotta stop."

"Oh really?" Kaiser leveled a feral grin his way. "Why, my mate?"

As a shudder worked through him, Kaiser attempted to breathe slow and deep—anything to get his body back under control. "Y-You're g-gonna make me c-come," he admitted, meeting Kaiser's gaze. Except, the man's smug smile accompanied by the way he rocked his hips against Arthur's did nothing to help calm him.

"It's okay, Arthur," Kaiser told him as he reached between their bodies. He cupped Arthur through his jeans, which yanked a gasp from him. Arching, Arthur felt his back pressed against something cool. "I'm gonna open these, and you're gonna show me how much you love my tentacle up your ass."

"I-I—"

Arthur blinked. For the first time in a while, he checked out his surroundings. They were in a bathroom stall.

As Arthur watched, Kaiser undid his fly and lowered his underwear, drawing out his throbbing shaft. Gasping at the cool air blowing over his heated flesh, he trembled against the door. As Kaiser wrapped his long fingers around his erection, he wiggled his tentacle in Arthur's chute.

"See," Kaiser purred, his expression lascivious. "We're safe and sound in the bathroom. Let yourself go." As he spoke, he worked Arthur's shaft. "Just relax and take the edge off."

Then Arthur felt something against his balls. Gaping, he peered past Kaiser's thick wrist. He spotted another tentacle curled up against his sack, cradling his balls and creating the most exquisite of friction.

Arthur moaned Kaiser's name as his body erupted in flames. His orgasm crashed over his senses. He trembled and twitched. Even though Kaiser quit jacking him, his orgasm continued due to the massaging his lover did to his prostate.

After Arthur wasn't certain how long, he felt something sliding over his overly sensitive dick. He peeled open his eyes, and panting harshly, he then peered downward. As he shivered and watched, Kaiser cleaned him up with some toilet paper.

Kaiser finished and tossed the soiled tissue into the toilet. At the same time, he eased his tentacle out of Arthur's chute. Even as he missed the sensation of fullness, he heaved a sigh of relief.

"Oh, god," Arthur mumbled, lifting his chin so he could meet Kaiser's gaze. He bit back a snicker as he took in his shifter's smug expression. "That was so evil, Kaiser."

Wrapping his arms back around him, Kaiser cradled his jaw in his left hand. "And, yet, you enjoyed every damn second of it."

"Yeah, I did," Arthur admitted.

After Kaiser pecked a kiss to his lips, he eased away. "Let's go wash up," he said, drawing Arthur away from the door. "Then we'll see how much crap we get from the guys."

Arthur snickered, figuring—at least from Jacob—there would be plenty.

Except, when Arthur allowed Kaiser to guide him from the bathroom stall, he froze. The sight of a gun being pointed at him could do that to a man. Holding the weapon was not the heavyset, dark-haired man from the alley. Instead, this was someone vaguely familiar to him.

After a second, Arthur cocked his head. "Peter?"

Peter's blond brows drew together as an angry flush filled his cheeks. "Oh, now you know my name?"

"Someone you know, my love?" Kaiser asked, his voice sounding deep while his tone was mild.

"He's not your love!" Peter shrieked. "He's mine!"

Then Peter swung the gun.

Kaiser stepped forward as he swung his right arm in an upward arc. Having had it behind Arthur, he'd already begun to shift it, so within seconds, it was plenty long enough to reach their attacker. He pivoted to the left as he stepped right, using the same move to push his mate to the side and out of the line of fire while making himself a more slender target.

As the gun went off, Kaiser slapped his tentacles against the human's wrist, driving his arm upward. The shattering of tile, along with the lack of pain, told him Peter — whoever the hell that was — had missed. He wrapped his tentacles around the man's wrist and shoved.

The gun went off again, and broken ceiling tiles rained upon them.

Rushing forward, Kaiser closed the distance between them. He raised his left arm and wrapped his hand around Peter's throat. Ignoring the ringing in his ears caused by the repeated release of the firearm, Kaiser drove the man backward until he slammed into the wall.

"What the fuck are you?" Peter cried, his wide-eyed gaze peering up at the tentacles that extended from Kaiser's elbow instead of his arm. "Shit! You're a freak!"

As Peter wriggled and tried to yank away, the gun in his hand clicking since he continued to pull the trigger, Kaiser just shook his head. He carefully reformed his hand as he peered over his shoulder at Arthur. "Are you okay, my mate?"

"I said he's mine!" Peter screamed before he started trying to kick Kaiser in the shins. "And no freak is gonna take him from me."

Kaiser lifted a knee and slammed it into the flailing man's balls.

Peter squeaked, his eyes rounding. Then he moaned as his body tried to hunch in on itself.

With his arm back to human form, Kaiser released Peter, who immediately slumped to the floor. Stepping on the gun, he kept the weapon pinned to the floor. As soon as Peter released it, he kicked it across the floor.

Their attacker curled into a fetal position. "I'm gonna have you put away for this," the man whined, cupping himself. "You're gonna be locked up, and I'm gonna get my man."

Kaiser sighed as he rolled his eyes. The guy was truly delusional. Holding out his hand for Arthur, he wiggled his fingers.

To Kaiser's pleasure, Arthur immediately slammed into his side, wrapping his arms around him.

"Are you okay, Arthur?" Kaiser murmured as he pressed a kiss to his temple. "Are you injured?"

"I'm fine," Arthur replied, rubbing his hands over Kaiser's chest. "What about you?"

"I'm good," Kaiser assured, then pulled out his phone and shot off a text to Dare. "You should call Detective Mirrins, handsome," he urged as he turned his attention back to a moaning Peter. "And maybe tell me who this is?"

"That's Peter Fletcher," Arthur told him as he pulled out his phone and began pushing buttons. "He works in my company's accounting department." Then his eyes widened. "Damn! I think the fat guy who tried to abduct me is his stepfather. I remember seeing his picture once."

"Mister Nesky? Whose stepfather. What's going on, sir?"

Obviously, Arthur hadn't even realized the detective had picked up.

Arthur began to explain to Detective Mirrins what happened just as Dare and Pisces shoved into the bathroom. They quickly took over watching Peter, so Kaiser urged his mate to the other side of the bathroom. With his heightened hearing, Kaiser easily made out the detective's reassurance that he was on his way.

There was a knock on the door, which Dare answered. Whoever it was seemed suitably cowed by the huge, dark-skinned octopus shifter, and he said he could hold it. A few seconds later, one of the bouncers showed up.

Dare let that man—a dark-haired tanned-skinned human—into the bathroom, and Kaiser explained what was happening. The bouncer, who introduced himself as Seth, said he would put up a sign and show everyone to the women's restroom. He also shot a text to whoever was bouncing the door, ordering them to watch for the detective.

Once they were alone again, Arthur whispered, "Aren't you worried about what might happen if Peter tells about what he saw?" He pointed at Kaiser's arm. "Your tentacles?"

Winking, Kaiser replied, "The great thing about being branded a crazy stalker is that no one will believe a word he says." He smirked as he waggled his brows. "Especially something so outlandish as a rich businessman's arm turning into tentacles."

Ten minutes later, where they weren't disturbed—other than Peter's continued claims that Arthur was his and he would make certain Kaiser would go to jail for assaulting him—Detective Mirrins arrived.

Two hours later, back at Arthur's condo, Kaiser wrapped his arms around his naked mate. He tugged Arthur close to him, flushing their naked bodies together. After drawing his human's comforter up their bodies, Kaiser let out a long breath, relaxing.

"So . . . it's over?" Arthur asked softly.

Kaiser nodded. "It's over. I talked with Detective Mirrins while you were in the shower. Peter's stepfather was picked up at a bar by a beat cop thirty minutes ago."

"Why did Peter's stepdad try to kidnap me?" Arthur asked, tipping his head back where it rested on Kaiser's chest so he could meet his gaze. "I mean, I get that Peter has a mental problem and for some reason became fixated on me, but what's with the stepdad?"

"Money," Kaiser revealed, grimacing. "He lost his job this past fall and has been doing odd jobs for cash." As much as Kaiser would have preferred to scrub Arthur himself, his mate had told him he'd needed a few minutes to decompress, so he'd given it to his human. Kaiser knew he would do damn near anything for the man. Besides, Kaiser was glad he hadn't missed the detective's call. "Peter paid his stepdad a grand to try to kidnap you. Even provided the chloroform."

"Shit." Arthur cuddled closer to Kaiser.

"Anyway, with the creepy collage Peter had created of you in his bedroom, along with the pictures all over the walls, the table with more cut-out letters for notes, plus the blood from the cat he killed still on the garage floor, Detective Mirrins has plenty of evidence against Peter." Kaiser threaded his fingers through Arthur's hair. "He won't be bothering you again."

"Thank god." Then Arthur smiled up at Kaiser. "I guess that only leads me to one conclusion."

Spotting the change in Arthur's expression and the shift in his scent, Kaiser arched one brow as he smirked. "Oh?" The heady fragrance of Arthur's growing arousal filled his nostrils, and his voice deepened as he asked, "And what's that?"

Arthur arched one eyebrow, his expression imperious. "How long do you think it will take you and your shifters to help me move in with you at our new cottage on the beach or our flat at *World of Aquatica*?"

Kaiser groaned. His cock jerked as he processed his mate's words. *Our new cottage. Our flat.* He sure liked the sounds of that.

Chuckling huskily, Kaiser rolled Arthur until his human lay sprawled under him. "That all depends on you." As he spoke, he slid his hand downward.

"On me?" Arthur's voice took on a breathy quality. "Me how?"

Unable to help himself, Kaiser began to rock his hips, frotting against Arthur's answering erection. He shifted his hand once again, using his tentacles to seek out his human's opening. When Kaiser pushed his appendages into Arthur's body, drawing a bliss-filled groan from his mate, he grinned widely.

"It depends on how many times I can fuck you through the mattress tonight, so then maybe I can manage to allow you out of bed in the morning."

Arthur moaned and wrapped his legs around Kaiser's waist. He wound his arms around his shoulders. Clinging to him, he rocked into Kaiser's tentacles' touches, grinding his dick against Kaiser's own in the process.

"Then you'd better get started," Arthur urged, lifting his head to capture Kaiser's lips.

Kaiser was more than on board with that . . . so he did.

ABOUT THE AUTHOR

Charlie started writing fantasy when she was eight, and after stumbling onto her first erotic romance at age nineteen, she realized her true calling. She now focuses on writing gay erotic romance, normally of the paranormal variety, with heroes of all kinds. With the help and support of her husband, Charlie finally fulfilled one of her life-long goals . . . move to acreage with her horses. You can often find her curled up with her laptop and a cup of tea or glass of wine, creating her next adventure. Charlie enjoys exploring the mountains of her new Oregon home on horseback, 4-wheeler, or motorcycle.

She can be reached at ch.richards2010@yahoo.com
Or visit her at www.charlie-richards.com